CROSSING LIMBO

Deep Moments, Shallow Lives

SHANE JOSEPH

Crossing Limbo

Print ISBN: 978-1-927882-37-5

Reprinted with permission:
"Waiting for the Train", *Hill Spirits II*, Blue Denim Press, April 2015, Cobourg.
"Mists of Memory", *Ten Stories High Vol. 15*, Canadian Authors Association Niagara Branch, 2015, St. Catharines.

Library and Archives Canada Cataloguing in Publication

Joseph, Shane, 1955-
[Short stories. Selections]
    Crossing limbo : deep moments, shallow lives / Shane Joseph.

Short stories.
Reprint. Originally published: Cobourg, Ontario: Morning Rain Publishing, 2017.
Issued in print and electronic formats.
ISBN 978-1-927882-37-5 (softcover).--ISBN 978-1-927882-38-2 (Kindle).--ISBN 978-1-927882-39-9 (EPUB)

        I. Title.

PS8619.O846A6 2018   C813'.6   C2018-905357-7
                                         C2018-905358-5

OTHER WORKS BY SHANE JOSEPH

<u>Novels</u>

Redemption in Paradise
After the Flood
The Ulysses Man
In the Shadow of the Conquistador

<u>Short Story Collections</u>

Fringe Dwellers
Paradise Revisited

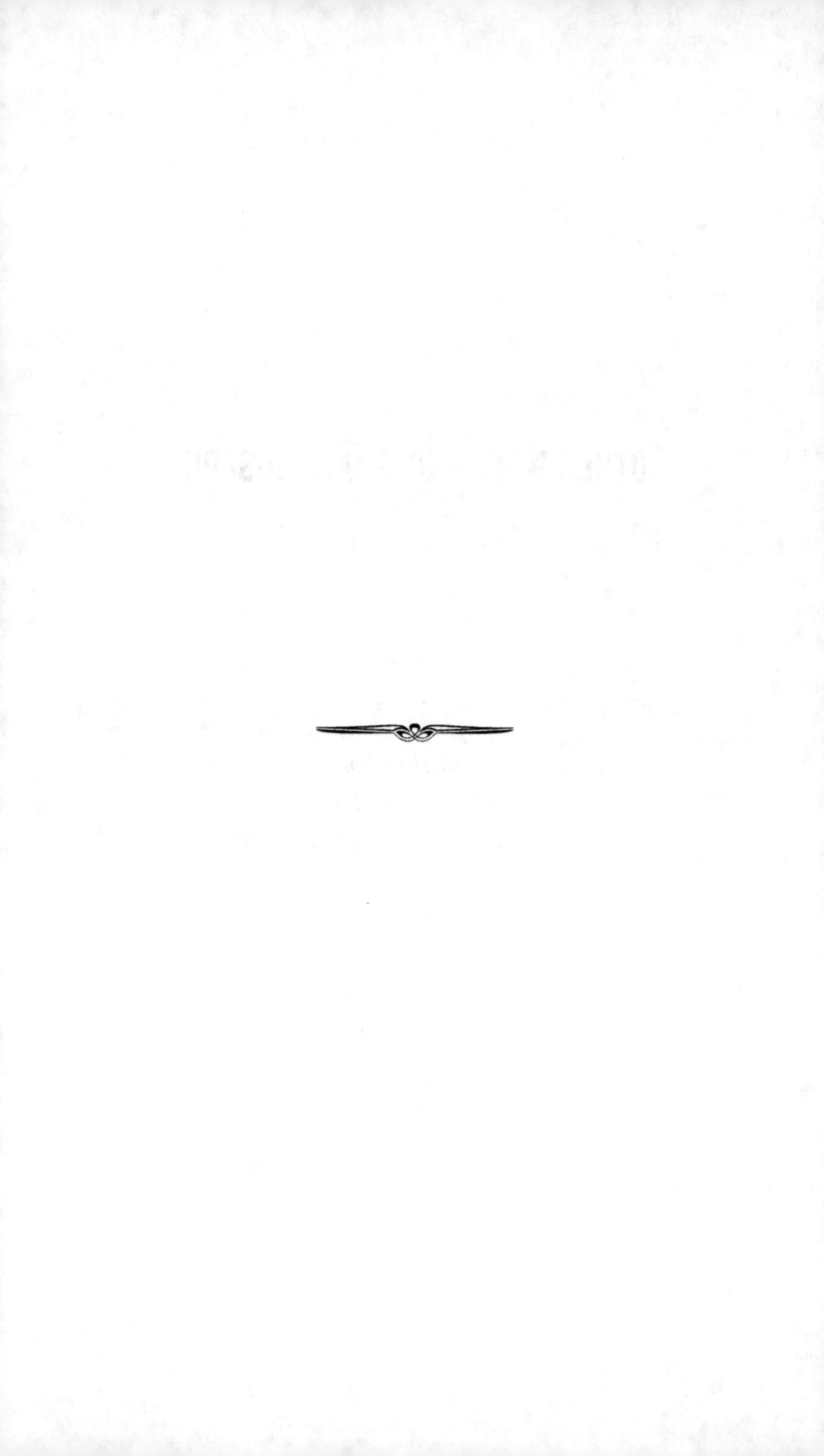

ACKNOWLEDGEMENTS

Many thanks to early readers of the manuscript who read the stories within, either as singles or as a collection, and who provided me with valuable feedback: members of The Pollard Group of Writers, The East End Writers Group, The Parliament Writers Group, Richard Pope, Ben Antao, Dessy Pavlova, Richard Joseph, and Michael Daly.

To the fine team at Morning Rain Publishing: Jennifer Jaquith, Jaclyn Brown, and Jo Kasunic, it was a pleasure to work with you.

To my wife, Sarah, for putting up with my long absences as I wrestled with these somewhat unfortunate and slightly unsavoury characters, following their lives, and guiding them across Limbo. Sometimes I succeeded in getting them to the other side, sometimes... well, you be the judge.

Shane Joseph
2017

We made our way across the lonely plain, like one
returning to a lost pathway, who, till he finds it, seems to
move in vain.

Purgatorio, Dante, Canto 1, 118

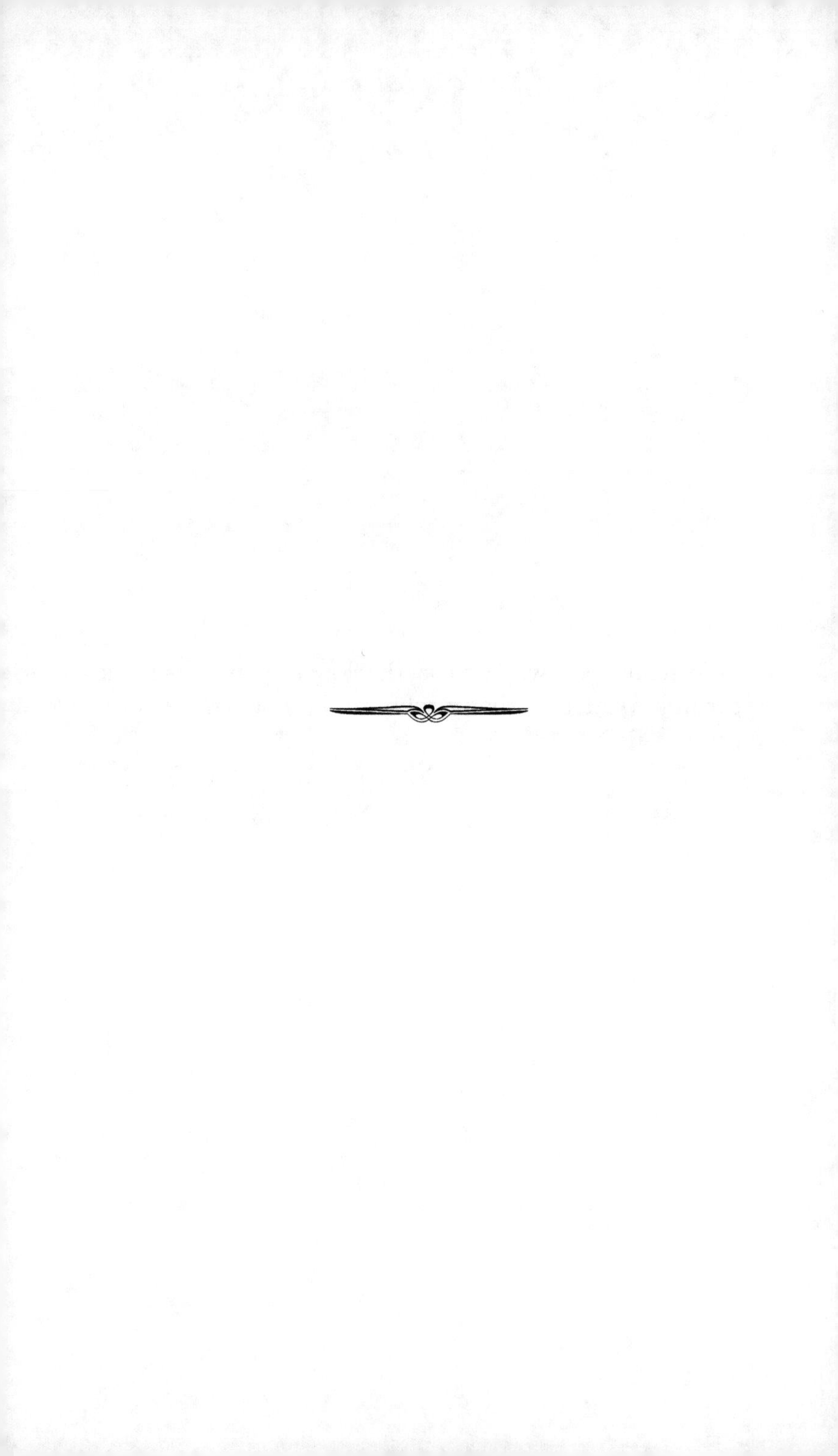

CONTENTS

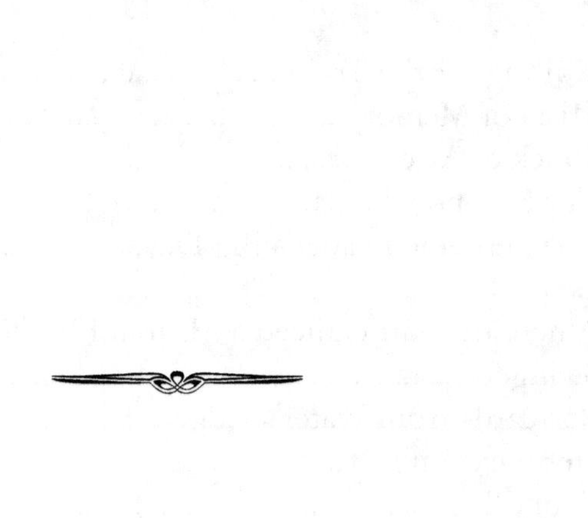

WAITING FOR THE TRAIN

He limped down the pathway between the rows of houses, approaching the water. This new estate had taken over his small community, distorting home prices, bringing newcomers, and appending the town as another suburb of the pulsing city that lay hidden behind the curve of the lake. The cancer in his leg had leached into the bone, a slow but relentless crawl, like the urbanization he had once tried to escape when he had fled the city. *There is no escape.* Then he heard the train whistle, a luring siren. *There is...*

He paused for breath; his heart was not so good anymore, and he had forgotten to take his pills. But it didn't matter now. None of those multi-coloured, multi-sized potions he took for a variety of ailments mattered anymore. One for high-blood pressure, one for cholesterol, one to thin his blood, one for pain, one for his ulcer, the other for his prostate, ointments for his hemorrhoids, and sprays for his lungs and nasal passages weakened by years of inhaling polluted city air, carpet dust, and pollens.

The train howled as it roared past, like a dragon from one of his books, eliminating anything in its path, hauling the nation's goods from east to west and back, and oblivious to the pollution it brought to the tiny towns it cut through on its relentless mission. Recently, an entire community had been wiped out in Lac Mégantic, Quebec when a parked train had woken up and decided to roll back into the little town, unleashing its toxic cargo among sleeping inhabitants. Tonight, the train would be his saviour.

When he came to the embankment, the last of the carriages were moving away, heading west; the whistle was blowing faintly ahead of the string of black cylindrical rail cars. He would take the next one, and there were plenty to choose from because both national rail lines ran parallel to each other, a few yards apart, on this stretch of their trans-Canadian journey. In the dark, beyond the lines, the waves of Lake Ontario lapped the shore; the wind was up tonight, and so was the moon, casting an eerie glow on the lush foliage that had yet to wilt in the summer heat.

He used a flashlight to find his footing and inch down the embankment. Midway, his weak foot slipped, and he slid, landing on his back at the stony bottom. Pain shot up him, starting from the cancerous knee, travelling through his body, and exiting in a muffled scream through bared lips.

He crawled over the last stretch to within a couple of feet of the CN track and rolled over on his back to catch his breath. The moon looked benignly upon him, summoning him. In the last year, this glowing orb, whenever it chose to show itself, had been his only companion: an entity he could talk to, particularly on nights when the insomnia had him in an unrelenting vice. *Damn! I used to run up these hills for hours just for exercise only a few years ago. How quickly we decay when purpose is lost.*

He turned on his side. Something moved between the CP track and the lakeshore. He shone his torch and caught what looked like a bundle of clothes. He laughed hoarsely. *A scarecrow from the fields, transplanted to the tracks—perhaps to scare away the trains!*

Then, the bundle moved, and he saw the girl.

She would do it tonight. She was resolved. Dashing her cell phone to pieces so those horrible images would not plague her anymore was the act of defiance that told her she could do this. She had been careful to collect the shattered pieces of the mobile device from her bedroom and deposit them in a municipal garbage container on her way down to the lake—she did not want Mom and her boyfriend finding out until... until afterwards.

No more calls from those bitches she had once called friends.

"Hey Rita, we saw you on the Tube. Didn't know you gave head so well."

No one had seen the knife held to her back, forcing her to comply.

Home offered no solace. She had never known her father who had been "out West" since she could remember. Her mother was too busy trying to look attractive for her boyfriend who was ten years younger. Brad gave Rita the salacious eye when he'd had one too many beers, especially when the Leafs lost to the Habs, and he had that "I want revenge" look on his face. She locked her bedroom door on those nights and heard Mom take the brunt of his frustration in the adjoining room. Mom would apply extra rouge and make-up and avoided her gaze the following morning. "What do you expect a single mom bagging groceries to do, huh?"

Her world had shrunk after that infamous sleepover party, when her friend Sandy had invited "the boys" over for the night. Sandy's parents had gone out of town. At first, it had been fun—beer and dancing to techno music. But then the ecstasy had emerged… and the knife… and the party had taken on a sinister tone. She had been too drunk to figure out whether this was a game or the beginning of the end of her life. Her friends had shunned her on the morning after; the teachers began looking at her strangely. Mom's only comment was that she should "get over it and move on and not go for any of those wild parties again."

The world had closed in. Sleeping pills hadn't helped. When she had OD'd at home, they rushed her to the hospital and had her stomach pumped. That damned counsellor who was assigned to her was a bigger bitch than her school teacher or Mom. No, she had to do this away from home and school, away from the narrow confines of her sheltered life. This act of defiance had given her a sudden boost of energy she had not felt in months.

She had watched the old man come down the embankment or, more appropriately, fall down. He seemed to be in pain, just as she was. She had wanted to rush to his aid but held back. He shone his flashlight in her face.

"Stop," she yelled.

"Stop what?"

"Shining that fucking light in my face."

The flashlight went out, leaving her in a halo of blindness. His shape started to re-emerge as the circle shrank.

"What are you doing this time of night?" he called out. His voice was raspy, protective. He sounded too old and ill to be dangerous.

"It's a good night to die," she said. She wanted to shock the old coot.

He chuckled. "Didn't know I was going to have spectators."

She suddenly realized why he was there. "I didn't, either."

He went silent. The flashlight came on again, trailing up from her feet and stopping short at her neck. "You're too young."

"Like, what's your reason? The nursing home not keeping you medicated?"

"I've got *too many* medications. And I live in my own apartment. What's yours?"

The flashlight went out. They only had the moonlight, but she did not need the glow for their voices had connected on a wavelength that needed no illumination.

What's mine? "Everything's fucked-up. School, home... everything."

"Ah—that."

"Don't patronize me."

"You pregnant?"

"No! They have morning-after pills for that."

"Then what you got to die about? You look healthy."

"Have you heard about Facebook and YouTube and Twitter?"

"Oh yes. I never use them."

"They made a video." She began sobbing.

He wanted to go over the tracks and comfort her. Hold her in his arms like the daughter he had never had, the family he'd had no time and opportunity to create. An invisible gulf separated them, however, a limbo created by generation, experience, and hurt. He dragged himself over the steel track on his side, catching his lame foot between the ties. *Shit. I'm in no position to help now. But I'm in perfect position for the train.*

"I'd come over if I could," he apologized. "But it looks like I'm kinda stuck."

Her sobbing turned to laughter. "You won't make a gallant knight." Her voice had a shrill treble, as if hysteria lurked in the higher octave.

He laughed, too, resignedly. "I guess not. I make better road kill... or rail kill."

She rose, took a deep breath, and sprawled awkwardly over the other track beside him. He smelled her trace of stale perfume mixed with the sour scent of fear.

"We could toss a coin for which train comes first— yours or mine. Or which one is delayed."

"Shut up."

"They say the neck is the best part to place on the steel. Sort of like the guillotine."

"I can't stand your jokes anymore," she screamed. She was hugging the rails as if scared she would change her mind. He saw her pale hair in the moonlight. She had a pretty face. She couldn't be more than 16.

"I wrote kids' books for a living," he said, looking up at the moon. "Some of my stuff was read in schools, once."

She had turned on her back too and was following his gaze. "What's your name?" Their voices bounced off the moon at each other.

He told her his name.

"Really?" She sat upright. The tenseness was replaced by curiosity. "I read your books in grade six. I thought you had died after *The Prisoner on Hemlock Hill*."

"Betcha your parents read them in grade six, too. They don't read them in grade six anymore. They read smart phones now and that Twitter stuff."

"Is that why you stopped writing?"

"When you lose your audience, you lose purpose. Then the ailments take over."

"I wish I could write."

"Why don't you? You have a story. Otherwise you wouldn't be here tonight. You can't leave the stage until the story is told."

She lay back on the track, and they remained silent, staring up at the moon. Her hurried breathing slowed. Then she sighed. "My story was told on YouTube."

"Someone else's warped version of it. They call that bullshit Reality TV. I am more interested in the author's authentic voice."

"Like, who will believe me?"

"When you write it with conviction, they will believe you even if you have to convert it into a fairy tale. You know that *Prisoner on Hemlock Hill*? That was me in boarding school when the bigger boys and the Fathers pursued me for sex. I turned the trauma into a children's story by taking the grimy stuff out and substituting gremlins and dragons for the real bastards. Now, those little pricks in grade six will only read it if I put the reality back."

A train whistle blew in the distance.

"That'd be my train," he said. "My track is vibrating."

"Omigod! So's mine." She was up and tugging on his coat.

"What are you doing?"

"Getting you out of here."

"So I can write another book?"

"So you can write mine."

"Leave me be. I'm done with writing. I've written all the stories I need to write. Get out of here and write your own."

Her grip was strong, and he felt his foot come loose from between the ties. He felt needed as she dragged him across the track. He hadn't felt this way since his books had started to fade from the limelight. He yielded to her pulling. She stumbled in the dark and they both tumbled to the ground again—this time across the other track.

"Fuck!" she screamed. "It's coming down this one." Ahead, a light glowed, and the whistle went off louder. The track rattled.

He grabbed her foot and tried to push her out of the path of the oncoming train, but she held onto him so tight they both rolled over the steel and down the slope towards the beach. The train whistled, and the roar was deafening. They had lost their grip on each other, but he felt her presence somewhere off to his right. Breathless, and slumped to the ground a few feet away from the track, he tried to crawl back up. He thought he heard someone yell from the passing cab. "Hey, watch it, you drunken bastard!"

She had crawled up to him, and he instinctively drew her into his embrace as the train cleared overhead, receding into the night. She was sobbing again, in relief, and she held onto him.

"Hush, my dear. We missed our train."

"I chickened out."

"Life won over."

"For you, too?"

It was nice holding onto her like this, under the moonlight. He couldn't remember the last time he had been this close to another human. Only in his books had he been engaged in other people's lives.

"Maybe, I could help you write your story," he said.

"You will?"

"Then we will not have to catch another train until we finish. Anyway, I think that engine driver will have phoned the police by now, and they'll be out here soon, before the next train comes. Like how they pick up druggies and drunks."

"I could get you home before that," she said, helping him rise to his feet.

"That would be nice." He dusted the sand off his clothes. "I am done with excitement tonight."

"Me too."

She helped him limp home under the moonlight and gave him a hug opposite his apartment building.

"You'll come tomorrow?" he asked. "We can start chapter one. And we have to hurry." He tapped his leg. "This poison spreads pretty fast."

There was a lot of sad stuff to get through, but she felt she could tell it to him. They had been to a very bad place and back again, a place her mom would never accompany her to. And she would stay with him as he slid into the other abyss that had opened up inside his leg.

"And you won't go back to those tracks until you finish?" he asked expectantly.

"I won't leave the stage until the story is told," she promised.

MISTS OF MEMORY

The two old men were placed beside each other in the sunroom for their daily ingestion of natural Vitamin D. "Watch them closely," said the doctor to Wilf. "This is when they go into the dangerous stage..."

Abe thought the man in the wheelchair next to him looked familiar; his white gloves stoked a memory. Wasn't he the guy who had come in yesterday, or was it last week? Whenever. This was the best time of day for conversation: when the post-breakfast meds kicked in and lucidity was at its peak. Their conversation would be forgotten by dinnertime.

"*Sind sie aus Deutschland?*" Abe's mother tongue was still holding as he continued to lose the English he had learned as an adult. How did he know the man was German? Another memory somewhere?

"*Ja.*"

Abe continued in German. It was a relief to find someone who spoke the language in this country that had played on the other side. "You fought in the war?"

"*Ja.* And you?"

"*Nein*. I fought for the British."

The other man's eyes narrowed. He remained silent, his toothless gums chewing some invisible cud.

Abe explained, "I didn't agree with Hitler. Not after he set up the deathcamps."

"Then you must be a Jew sympathizer."

"I am a Jew and a German."

"And you betrayed the Fatherland."

"Were you a Nazi?"

The other man chewed some more. "We never talked about it after the war. Got you in trouble."

"What's your name?"

"Henry. What's yours?"

Abe didn't reply for he had temporarily forgotten his name.

Henry added, as if remembering something, "The British had death camps too—in the Boer War."

They sat in silence for the rest of their time in the sunroom, until the attendants came to wheel them away.

The fog came regularly now and took longer to leave. The surroundings faded, and he ran back in time to cling to whatever defined him as human. The past became more palpable than the present. It was a good refuge except the past held pain and loss and the murderous impulse to kill in order to right the enormous wrongs committed during that time. And then, mercifully, the fog would lift.

He was just coming back into the present when the door to his room opened, and the burly attendant, known as Wilf, wheeled an old man inside.

"Brought you some company, Abe," Wilf said and lifted the emaciated old man onto the unused bed of the double room. The man, who was wearing white gloves and a pyjama suit, lay still in the fetal position.

Abe had only recently moved into this room and was getting used to its landmarks; it was unlike his former room on the east wing where he had spent two years.

"Henry, stay right there, and I'll be back with your things," said Wilf, wheeling the empty chair away.

There was a change in the energy in the room, Abe sensed. As his mind had deteriorated, his senses had sharpened, and he could tell good vibes from bad ones. With Wilf, for instance, the vibes were all good. It wasn't so with the man in the other bed.

After a lapse of time, during which a minor haze swooped in and retreated, the door re-opened and Wilf returned with a small suitcase. He opened it, pulled out shirts, slacks, underwear, and a pair of shoes, and placed them inside the empty cupboard beside Henry's bed.

"Abe, take note. Your stuff is on the right side of the room, and Henry's, here, is on the left. Henry needs assistance, and the staff will help him with toileting, washing, dressing, etcetera."

"Does he talk?" Abe asked.

Wilf smiled. "He does. When he is in the mood. He gets cold easily, that's why he wears gloves. Right now, he has travelled from one nursing home to another, and he is exhausted."

"Why is he here? I don't need anyone but Esther."

"Esther?"

"My wife."

"Your wife died a long time ago, Abe. You told me that story."

"Everyone died."

"But you survived, Abe. You triumphed. You came to Canada and built a new life."

"Why is this man here?"

"The doctors say that patients... residents... like you and Henry, are better off with company. I think you will like Henry." Wilf gently retreated, clicking the door shut behind him.

Abe wheeled his chair over to Henry's cupboard and opened it. A man's possessions were signposts to his character, and yet the newcomer had no past, just clothes. No photographs, books, letters, souvenirs—just clothes. Abe hurried across to his side of the room and rummaged in his cupboard, pulling items out at random and in haste, as if he wanted to remind himself of his own history that was slowly being wiped clear. Out came the diaries, the yellowed letters from Esther that had trailed off into silence, Jeremiah's rubber duck, Sarah's cloth doll, Naomi's bonnet. His hands were full as he tried to hold onto every object, and they began to fall from his grasp. The more he tried, the more they fell, and soon he was holding onto a solitary diary with the rest strewn on the floor.

The man in the opposite bed had opened his eyes and was observing Abe. He spoke in a high-pitched voice, German accented, like Abe's. A shiver ran down Abe's spine—a recognizable voice from somewhere.

"You can't take them with you," Henry said.

"I've had them for a long time."

Henry grinned, displaying broken, tobacco-stained teeth. Then he closed his eyes; he had gone back to sleep.

Abe pressed the call-button to summon the attendant to help gather his fallen possessions.

On the second occasion, they met in the sunroom, their conversation drifted to Canada.

"When did you come to this country?" Abe asked.

"After the war, sometime. I do not remember."

"Do you have a family?"

"Nein."

"Job?"

"Many jobs. Security guard, mainly. And you?"

"Teacher. German translator. That sort of thing."

They sat silently for some time. The sun had gone behind a cloud, and the room was developing a chill.

"My family died in Birkenau," Abe said.

Henry nodded. He tugged on his gloves, pulled his blanket tighter around his feet, and shivered.

"It doesn't bother you? That we killed so many people?" Abe asked.

"Humans create and kill their own all the time. That is why I did not have a family. What's the use?"

The nurses arrived earlier that day, given the overcast sky. Abe was relieved to exit the conversation. He had no answer to Henry's question.

The fog returned thicker that evening, and Abe was lost in it....

Braun shoves the electrodes at his genitals, again. Abraham screams. He tells himself that very soon it will not matter. His balls will be fried, and they will have to find another place for pain to penetrate. The soles of his feet are already charred and dead. Fear beats logic, and he screams every time those electrodes come near him.

"Jew bastard, keep this up, and you will never have any more children."

"You killed the ones I had. I don't want your fucking pity."

Braun strikes with the back of his gloved hand, and Abraham slumps into a merciful delirium.

Water splashes over him, bringing relief to his parched body, waking him to the next chapter in this ordeal.

Braun comes into view. "Waltheimer, remember. We only need the name of your British contact. A name, and then you are free."

Free to die. "Fuck you!"

As the electrodes send their neutering barbs through his quivering body, Abraham forces his mind away to another time, when Esther wrote him those beautiful letters and always appended a small line from each of the children; Naomi could only manage a thumbprint. The letters had been smuggled to him while he worked the radio transmitter in Bremen for the Allies, letters hidden along with other memorabilia and waiting for him when he escaped this hell.

My Love—we miss you, and yet, your work is important. Naomi started walking yesterday. A real joy to see the first steps that will lead to those of a beautiful woman and a mother one day, we hope.

More soldiers in the village yesterday, going from door-to-door, asking to see ID badges. Jeremiah proudly displayed his, and the soldier patted him on the head. We hope that this time, too, will pass, and that I don't have to line up for hours to get a loaf of bread, that we can be normal Germans again like everyone else. We hope you return soon. We hope...

Hope dimmed when the letters slowed to a trickle, blamed on too many censors and checkpoints and on the massive manhunt for traitors of the Reich. Then the letters stopped.

"Heinrich," a voice from behind restrains Braun's next assault on his body. The Nazi doctor presiding over the torture doesn't think the prisoner can take much more today and says it aloud.

Braun is sweating, cursing this intransigent Jew who is allowing his body to be mutilated. Abraham grins through his pain. Victory, whatever that is, is imminent; Braun can rend his body, but he will never occupy his soul. A soldier enters the room bearing a paper, and there is a conference of voices behind him.

"Your wife is still alive, Waltheimer," Braun says, brandishing the paper in his hand.

"Bullshit! You killed them all."

"*Nein!* We have word that she works in a factory outside Birkenau. Your brats, unfortunately, went straight from the train to the gas chamber. But she is alive."

Esther alive? Or is this another trick? Braun has struck a blow more serious than those with the accursed electrodes.

"Give me proof."

"Give me a name first."

"Give me proof that she is alive."

"We don't bargain."

"Then, fuck you!"

Time passes. He has been in this room for how long he cannot tell. The stench is infernal for no one has removed the slop bucket that has overflowed. Boiled potatoes and water are pushed under the grate with decreasing frequency, but no one takes the empty plates away. He has to grab the food before the rats get to it and pile the empty dishes in a corner away from his cot. There is the drip of water somewhere, and he screams at night for it to shut off, as if that would shut off the pain in his body. The Chinese had picked their torture methods well, and now the Nazis have adapted them.

Braun is standing before him again, stretching out a crumpled piece of paper.

"Read," he commands.

It is a letter dated a week ago, in Esther's handwriting.

My dearest Abraham—I hope you are well. We were brought to the Birkenau camp by train. It was an arduous journey. I haven't seen the children. They were taken away in a group along with some older people to be showered, given new clothes, and sent to a special camp. We were told that they would be fed, treated well, and that there would be German teachers for the children. I have been assigned to work in the munitions factory. It is hard work, and I do not know how long I can last.

Yesterday, a commandant came to me and asked me to write this letter to you. They say that I will be released if you co-operate. I don't know what that means or where you are. I only hope that we will be together soon and re-united with the children.

My love,
Esther

Hope flickers in this dim, smelly cell. Will he ever have a chance of seeing his sweet Esther again? Reality takes over: they would never let him out of here, no matter what deal he cuts. If only he could ensure her safety...

He sees the tobacco-stained, uneven teeth of Braun in front of him.

"She must be released and sent to England. When I have proof, real proof, I will give you the name."

"You ask for too much."

"Talk to me when you have complied. In the meantime, I prefer the company of the rats."

Braun flushes crimson and stalks out of the cell.

The fog lifted, and he was staring at an old man wearing white gloves in the opposite bed.

"Who are you?"

"I'm Henry. You looked like you were in pain."

"I've been in pain all my life. Did you serve in Birkenau?"

Henry screwed his face. "I don't remember."

"The Russians came and liberated the camp. They were too late for my Esther."

Abe slipped back into the fog.

They have ignored him for two weeks: since the last electrocution. There is enough going on for distraction. The rumble of guns is getting closer. Loud explosions occur at night, and the drone of aircraft is constant. Sirens sound regularly, making sleep impossible with the accompanying shudder of anti-aircraft fire. Prisoners are being marched out of cells, and the moans of misery have diminished in the vicinity.

There isn't much remaining in him; perhaps they have left him to be mopped up with the slop and the garbage. The door bursts open, and framed in it is Braun, looking drunk, dishevelled, and distracted.

"Is she in England?" Abraham asks, betraying his hopefulness.

Braun pulls out a Luger from his holster and advances. "I am here to exterminate you, Waltheimer, like one of your friendly rats. You will go down as the only Jew who passed through my hands who was not smart enough to sing and save his hide."

"Where is Esther?"

"I don't know, and I don't give a damn! We have orders to evacuate, but I am not leaving until I give you what you deserve, you *arschloch*!"

There is a shrill whine followed by a brief pause, during which Braun's eyes widen in fear, and then the whole building explodes. Abraham later believed, for once in his life, his absent God had spoken in that moment.

The wall next to Braun collapses, and he is instantly buried under a pile of rubble; only the hand with the Luger sticks out and flexes as if determined to complete its job. The blast has thrown Abraham out of his cot and onto the floor, mere feet away from the buried Braun. His hands are all that remain functional, and he uses them to drag himself up the pile of broken concrete towards his tormentor. There is a deafening silence following the explosion, and the two men are all that move in this scene of devastation. Summoning all his strength, Abraham picks up a piece of concrete shrapnel, raises it high above his head, and brings it crashing down on the protruding arm, crushing bone and metal, and burying his torturer forever, he hopes.

Outside, sentries in the watchtowers have either fled or been killed. People are running for their lives, and no one stops to help fallen comrades. The sirens issue their plaintive wails, not of warning, but as laments for the dead and dying. Figures loom through the dust and cordite, their helmets identifying them as soldiers of the liberation forces. One soldier points to a cockroach-like figure, crawling on all fours out of a destroyed cell block, and like the insect, looking determined to escape the annihilation of man.

The man in the opposite bed was having a nightmare when the fog lifted this time. He howled and uttered curses in German in his sleep. Abe had forgotten the man's name again. The medications were losing their effectiveness, and the moments of fog had intensified as of late. When the cloud lifted, everyone in the vicinity was a stranger. Only the past was crystal clear.

Unable to sleep, and annoyed by his groaning roommate, Abe slid into his wheelchair in the half-lit room and wheeled over to the restless man's bed. He read the nameplate on the headboard: Henry Brown. He did not know a Henry Brown, but it triggered another name from the past.

Coming around the side of the bed he reached for the dreaming man's gloved right hand, and that seemed to calm Henry. *Why does he wear a glove?* Wilf had mentioned something about it, but Abe couldn't remember. The hand was familiar, and it triggered its own memory. Abe peeled back the glove, sensing what he would find. The fingers were deformed and scarred, as if they had been in an accident, or was it just old age? Abe grabbed a pillow. He would use it like that boulder of rubble from those many years ago. This time, he would finish the job, and there wouldn't be a trace. He placed the pillow on Henry's squirming face and was about to press down hard when the lights went on.

"Abe, what are you up to?" Wilf's brows were furrowed.

Abe let the pillow fall out of his hands. "Henry's having a rough night. So am I."

"Hmm. You both look like you need a topper on your meds. I'll talk to the doctor tomorrow." Wilf wheeled Abe over to his side of the room and strapped him into his bed. "For your safety," he said, giving Abe a funny look.

They sat in the sunroom, high on the increased dosage of medication, their conversation reduced to inane subjects like the weather; did they have strawberry jam for breakfast, or was it marmalade? Everything else was a blur.

"Good," said the doctor to Wilf, surveying his two patients as he paused outside the sunroom.

SHOCK & AWE

They became my family after Tommy's father, Bob, put on a civilian suit and went away in a van. Tommy read the vehicle's livery out with pride: International Security Experts. Every evening afterwards we watched TV; from the blurred images and sounds of terse newscasters, I gathered that there was a war going on in a place called Iraq, a sandy landscape similar to ours. Tommy announced that our side was winning. "Shock and Awe" was the approach being taken. I wondered if humans had borrowed that practice from the animal world. We did not do things in half measures: when we sprang on our prey, we did not give up until our opponent was dead.

Three months—as humans measure time—later, Tommy told me that his Daddy was not coming back because he had been killed in Iraq, and that the war was going to carry on for a long time, that it was no longer about WMDs but about oil. I tried to nuzzle Tommy that night when he broke the news, but he cried, took his father's rifle, and shot stones behind the house. Being a 12-year-old, he was rude to his mother for a while afterwards. Now that they had lost the head of their family, I had to protect them. I felt that these humans could not emulate us animals that well. "Shock and Awe" hadn't quite worked out as they had intended.

Tommy's mother, Linda, is half Apache, half white; she wears buckskins and jeans and rides on horseback about their property here on the rim of the desert. She rides to wear herself out; it's her way of grieving. I know because I ran like that every time they took my litter away "to sell it," as they said. It's like a part of you dies. I heard the Sheriff say these repeated losses made me a better hunter and gave me an edge. I became whole again when they brought Buster from Mr. Purdy's ranch, and he mounted me with passion and filled me with more pups. I liked mating with Buster when I was at my orneriest and couldn't think straight until his staff went between my legs; it calmed me down, dissolving my heat.

I had seen Linda like that with Tommy's father. When Bob brought me home from the Sheriff's office that first night, I was free to roam around the house. I crept up to the master bedroom and peeked through a crack in the door. I saw them mounting each other in turn with savage ferocity, clawing, crying, and sighing. I could smell the passion flowing between their bodies, trying to drown the morning when Bob was going away to protect those construction workers in Iraq—from where he never came back.

I crept away from their bedroom door, missing Buster, even though Mr. Purdy's homestead was next door. I also missed the Sheriff's office—hunting those bad people when I smelled drugs on them, watching the smarter ones trying to ditch their clothes that gave them away. I got them every time. I had even been trained to kill when necessary. After my last litter, I started to slow down, but not before I *nearly* killed that bad guy who pulled a gun on the Sheriff. I jumped to grab the dope dealer's weapon, missed my mark, and chomped on his balls instead; the guy collapsed in a howl, shooting his gun at the sky. After that incident, they said that I was a "risk" and needed a new home. So Bob, who was the best deputy on the force, brought me to his farm. My reward for solving the Sheriff's problem was being put out to pasture, like the old horses on this farm. I do not understand these humans' logic.

Now, I help around the farm, herding the chickens into their coops, shepherding the horses when they are released to graze, chasing away coyotes at night, catching the odd rattler. I watch the horses mate, bucking and thrashing around, and smell my own heat, missing Buster even more.

I smelt that same heat on Linda, the first time the suited man, Jim, came over, a few months after Bob died. Tommy stalked out of the house, jumped on his horse, and rode away in a trail of dust. I gave up chasing him and doubled back to the house. Linda was rocking on the swing seat on the porch; the man in the suit was beside her. She was drinking whiskey and laughing. I could see the hunger in his eyes too. They started applying their lips to each other, their tongues entwining. I thought they would fall off the swing and barked to protect her.

"Hush, Shep," Linda said curtly and resumed the spittle exchange. She then tugged the man by his belt and dragged him inside the house. "It's been a long time, Jim—too long."

I put my tail between my legs and slunk away, hoping Tommy had calmed down and would be heading home soon.

Don't get me wrong; Linda was generous. She fed me well: always the choicest food from the grocery store, though lately she was mixing it with leftovers. She kept a clean, but run-down house; the walls needed a coat of paint and the eavestroughs were broken. The family car made awful sounds—I was spoiled by having ridden around in the Sheriff's cruiser all the time. Linda drove Tommy to school every morning and picked him up in the afternoon. Sometimes she would take me along in the back seat, especially after her husband died. Tommy was always glad to see me after school. I seemed to be his only friend. After we got back to the house, we would roam around the gulch, a half-mile away, and track down rabbits whenever they came by. After those druggies, rabbits were a piece of cake. The laws of animals were easy to understand—the hierarchy ruled, and no one broke the rules, not even those at the bottom. By comparison, humans were more complicated—that's why they needed us to look after them. But since the forest fires started last year, the rabbits had gone somewhere else.

Only Buster and I prevailed. A week after I arrived at my new home, I saw him eyeing me on the southern end of the property line where Mr. Purdy's land bordered ours. My heart leaped when I saw him. Hope soared in me even though a barbed wire separated us. I paraded in front of him on my side of the fence, watching him ooze saliva on the ground and bark his head off, his staff erect and knocking against his belly repeatedly. I got a perverse sense of power from my act. I wanted to keep him salivating. It would only make our union juicier, whenever I was next in heat, and I knew it was only going to be a matter of time before that happened. Our pups fetched good money for the humans; the Sheriff had made a private income from me, although I couldn't do police work for him when I was with puppies.

Once, when I had ventured off to the western fence line, I saw the oil company workers—where that man in the suit worked—unloading their equipment. They had started digging there. No wonder the rabbits, lizards, and other wildlife had hightailed it!

Linda painted scenes of buttes rising on the western end of the ranch before they fell down to the ocean near the town. She created beautiful sunsets and highlighted the prickly Cholla cactus and misshapen Joshua trees, which even my blurred vision could make out. Twice a month, she would collect a batch of her paintings and drive away for two or three days. On those days, I looked after Tommy, when he'd be going to school and coming back, driven in Mr. Purdy's pick-up.

Mr. Purdy was getting kinda lame and old; he was always talking about selling and moving east, and I was scared that he would take Buster with him, or worse still, put him to sleep—these humans treated us like commodities, for all the loyalty we showed them.

During Linda's absences, Tommy and I rounded up the chickens in the evenings. Linda always stocked the fridge during her trips, so we ate well. Afterwards, I sat at Tommy's feet in the living room while he watched television but not about that horrible war, anymore. When Tommy avoided his schoolwork, I would bark non-stop until he pulled out his books. "You're worse than Ma," he shouted one day and threw a book at me.

When Linda returned, she looked happy, as if she had been having fun—the kind Buster and I used to have. She looked less stressed. And she brought back money, too, which she tossed triumphantly on the table. "We're good for another month, kiddo."

One day, Tommy and Linda got into an argument.

"There's never enough to look after this place," Tommy yelled. "The house is falling apart."

"The money from the paintings is chump change, Tommy—enough to get by—not enough to invest in this place."

"The ranch belonged to Dad's family. He would have looked after it if he was still alive."

Linda pointed a finger. "Your Dad was his only 'remaining family'—you get that? His only brother died in Operation Desert Storm. If he had the money to look after this place, your Dad would have never gone off to Iraq to fight this second war. I told him not to go, but he didn't listen—the 'man of the house' has to provide and all that shit."

"I'll work this land when I'm older."

"Oh no, you won't. *You* are going to college."

"But Dad's family always lived off the land."

"Times are a-changing. Jim's company has offered us half a million dollars for this place. It'll pay for your college and then some."

"You're going to sell?"

"Why not? It's of no use to us, other than to inspire paintings that people don't give a rat's ass for."

"We could sell Shep's pups if we mate her again. Dad said the Sheriff used to make good money on her."

"Go on—that's all we do—prostitute ourselves, sell our offspring. They used to do that in the reserves— young girls, pups in the hands of dirty old white men."

"I was trying to help!"

Tommy got up and stalked away from the dinner table. I crept out from under and followed him. He paused on the porch, looking at the horizon where an orange glow danced. Tommy had told me it was a flare the oilmen had lit that never went out. We walked down to the dried-up gulch, and Tommy kicked empty cans and stones at the bottom. I slid down the pebbly incline and nipped at his heels. I knew that it cheered him up. He ruffled my ears and smiled. I had taken his mind away from his mother, for now.

"Dad would never have sold," he said before we started back home.

Linda saddled her gelding that night and rode out. I stayed up for her, long after Tommy went to sleep. When she returned, the first cocks were crowing. She dragged herself into her room and fell on her bed and was asleep in minutes, fully clothed. Later, I heard her sobbing.

It wasn't long before Buster was brought over. We had a good time. Without the Sheriff scheduling our regular mating sessions with Mr. Purdy, things had fallen off a bit in the last year. Buster hadn't lost any of his charm; he pounced on me the moment he sniffed me. He came soon, too, filling me with his seed, getting entwined in me. His rod would remain stiff and only soften with time—or if our owners opened the water hose on us.

Later, I went to old man Purdy's pick-up to say goodbye. Buster was prowling about inside the vehicle, as if he was looking for a second inning with me. We growled at each other. I liked Buster's discomfort. It made me feel needed.

"Aw let 'em at it again," Mr. Purdy said, opening the truck's gate and letting Buster out once more. My panting lover promptly mounted me without permission. I was used to it and liked it. "At least someone is having fun these days," Mr. Purdy said approvingly.

I was having so much fun that I almost didn't hear his next words to Linda.

"They offer to buy your place yet?" he asked, putting a plug of tobacco in his mouth.

"All the time," she replied. "And yours?"

"Jim says he'll pay me a quarter million." Mr. Purdy chewed and spat a stream of brown spittle.

"Given the size of your spread, I think that would be a fair offer," she said.

"Yeah, but is *that* the price? I'd like another company to make a competing offer. Then we'll know what the *real* price is."

"You should take his offer. You keep talking about selling up and moving."

"As long as my pond doesn't go dry I can still raise livestock."

"But the water levels have been going down with this drought."

"You know, there are days when I feel like quitting. Then I think of Bob Senior, your father-in-law. Him and I bought these spreads after the second world war. He never quit. Died riding herd over by Dead Man's Canyon."

"He should have been more careful."

"You're half-native. Don't the land pull you?"

"I'm half-white, too. I was heading to L.A. to try my hand at the movies when I met Bob. I'm still trying to get to L.A."

Mr. Purdy slapped his hips and surveyed Linda— her T-shirt was tight, and her large nipples were sharply outlined against it.

"You're still an attractive woman. If I were twenty years younger, I would have given that oilman a run for his money."

Linda smiled, looking at Mr. Purdy the same way I looked at Buster from my side of the fence sometimes, goading him on.

"It gets very lonely up here on this ranch. I'm grateful for Jim's company."

Buster had gone limp inside me. He withdrew his staff, which hung like a bloody entrail between his legs.

"Time to get him back," Mr. Purdy said, rubbing Buster's neck and steering him towards the pick-up.

Jim came around a lot more after that first time he and Linda had mated. He began to stay over, and on those nights, Tommy slept in the barn. I kept my young master company as Jim and Linda made a lot of noise together; she loved to scream, and he would whinny like a horse. Linda would look at her lover the next morning with hungry adoration.

"Mom wants me to be nice, but I don't trust him," Tommy said to me one night. He talked to me a lot. He probably was the only one who *knew* that we were not "dumb animals" as Mr. Purdy called us. He'd taught me things—like colours, which I associated with shades of light.

"Jim is going to be rich one day, she says," Tommy carried on. "Owns his own oil company and is buying up land where he thinks there are deposits before the bigger guys can grab them. Mr. Purdy says he's just a squatter, buying and holding, waiting for the price to go up, and then selling to the highest bidder. Mr. Purdy says he's no oilman. I wish Mom would see it that way." Tommy banged his fist into the barn wall and cried in pain.

I nuzzled closer and licked his bruised fingers. When Tommy's pain subsided, he put his arm around me, and soon he was snoring; my heartbeat matched his. Before my pups were birthed, our heartbeats were often synchronised. As I had never seen my offspring for longer than a few weeks, this was the closest I had gotten to play mother. Tommy and I were kindred spirits.

I knew things had taken a turn for the worse when I missed seeing Buster come to the fence to bark at me. We couldn't creep through the fence without getting hurt on the barbed wire, so we contented ourselves with looking and barking. Ever since I had moved to the ranch, this was a ritual we had engaged in, especially when the sun was hot overhead. For two whole weeks he never came. I travelled the fence line trying to catch his scent; it was faint in places. One day, I decided to be reckless and did something that Buster could never do: I crept under the fence, tearing my back on the barbs in my hurry. Blood soaked into my fur as I edged onto Mr. Purdy's property. I skirted the ridge and chased a lizard up to the summit. The little guy slipped into a hole under a rock that I couldn't get past. Losing interest, I moved on. The scratch on my back began to hurt, and I couldn't reach to lick it. The sun made the pain worse. I raced down the other side of the hill and neared a large area of water—this had to be Mr. Purdy's pond. There were no animal scents—surprising, given the heat. But as I came by the water's edge I got Buster's smell again, mingled with human ones. His scent led right into the water, and I jumped in, expecting him to pop his head from below the surface and surprise me. I soaked in the cool water, ridding myself of the caked blood. The pain on my back started to ease. I swam some more, staying away from the middle of the pond that was deep and scary.

I could not smell Buster anymore. I came out shaking off drops of water tinged with blood and circled the pond, trying to catch his scent from where he could have re-surfaced. Nothing. I widened my arc. Had he stepped out of the pond in the same place he'd gone in? What were the humans doing with him? Taking him for a bath? There were two scents: one acrid and sour and the other a slight perfume that was familiar.

That was when I began to detect *another smell.* The smell of rotting animal. It was all over me and getting stronger as I dried in the sun. I rolled over in the soft sand at the water's edge, trying to be rid of the awful stench. But it only magnified as my mind tried to quell the dreadful knowledge creeping up on me. I darted away from the pond to stay ahead of the anger and panic. Panting and gasping in my confused state, I arrived back at the line between Mr. Purdy's property and ours. I had to get back through the fence.

A jeep roared over the hill with several passengers inside. They spotted me and drove over. I was trapped with the fence behind me and the vehicle in front—trespassing.

"Shep!" It was Mr. Purdy, sounding worried. "What are you doing on this side?"

I put my head down and looked humble. I must have looked awful—wet, muddy, and bloody. And frightened.

"What have you done to yourself, girl?" Mr. Purdy patted me gently. "Get in. We've got some unpleasant business ahead of us, I'm afraid. I can't have you running around all scared."

He helped me inside the vehicle. There were two other guys in the back, surrounded by rubber body suits and heavy gear. We drove over the ridge, back to the pond. The two men got into their rubber suits, hoisted metal canisters onto their backs, attached masks to their faces, stuck pipes in their mouths, waded into the water, and disappeared from view. They were gone about fifteen minutes. Mr. Purdy sat, sighing and smoking his smelly cigar.

When the men came out of the water they were carrying Buster's dead body between them.

"This is the final blow, Shep," was all Mr. Purdy said. "The final blow!"

I barked and jumped out of the jeep, running towards Buster's lifeless body. I circled Buster, sniffing, willing him to rise and mount me, or show some sign of life. He just lay there, wet, shrivelled, and uninterested. I howled like crazy and ran, heading back for the fence, squeezing through and feeling my back rip again—really bad this time. I *sought* the hurt, running through blinding pain with blood trailing behind me. I felt weak. As I staggered over the last hill, Linda and Tommy were pulling up in the car in front of the farmhouse.

Tommy zoomed in, his satchel of school books over his shoulder. "Shep, what the heck's gotten into you?"

I was barking and shaking, scattering gobs of blood on the ground and cursing humans for not understanding my language at a time like this.

They managed to get me into the barn, and Linda applied ointment to my back while I fell into an exhausted stupor.

"We have to get her to the vet. These wounds will get infected." Tommy said.

His mother jumped in. "We don't have money for vets. I'll drive around to Mr. Purdy's. He's dealt with lots of these in the past."

Linda was gone a couple of hours. When she returned, Mr. Purdy was with her. Tommy had tethered me with a leash—unusual. I recalled the last time I had been restrained: in the Sheriff's office, after I bit that druggie's balls.

Mr. Purdy stuck a needle into me, and I nearly broke my moorings at the sharp stab of pain. Then he threw some liquid on my wounds, and it burned. He followed it with a cream that numbed.

"At least she's alive. Buster wasn't so lucky."

"What happened?" Tommy asked.

"He drowned in the pond," Linda said flatly. "Dumb animal went right into the middle and couldn't get back."

"And I thought he had gone looking for a bitch in heat," Mr. Purdy said, putting away his things. "He's been dead several days—enough to poison the pond."

Mr. Purdy stayed for dinner. Tommy unleashed me when he saw that I was stable. I ambled outside the front door, looking towards the dying rays of the sun—orange, as Tommy had told me—blurry and large like a big warning sign up ahead. My loneliness was worse than when my pups were taken from me. Them, I hardly knew; Buster I had known intimately. I wished Tommy would come and nuzzle me for a change.

There were more important things for my human masters to discuss that night. Their conversation drifted over to me.

"I should have accepted Jim's offer," Mr. Purdy said, taking a swig from the whiskey Linda had offered him. "He came to see me before you arrived. His offer is down to half the original price now."

Tommy erupted. "He doesn't waste time profiting from your bad luck."

Linda intervened. "That's still a good offer, considering all the work you would have to do to drain the pond and re-flood it. And what's your livestock going to do in the meantime?"

"I don't have many options. I have no money for a cleanup. Jim's offer was based on the oil in my land, not on my cattle. The oil potential has not changed, so why this price drop?"

"Why don't you get another oil company to check things out?" Linda said.

"It takes time for sampling, decision making, and all that. These oil giants don't move as fast as Jim. And if they know I'm sitting on a measly one-hundred-and-twenty-five-thousand-dollar offer, with time running out, I don't think they'll come up with much more."

"How much time *do* you have?" Linda asked.

"I am going to round up the herd tomorrow. They are still under-grown at this time. Harry Burgess from Two Fork Ranch has offered to buy them off me and raise them to maturity. I'll be back in ten days. By then, I have to decide."

"I'll talk to Jim in the meantime," Linda said, and I could see her jaw set, and her eyes staring out the window.

When he got out of the black car, he looked determined and confident. His face was craggy, his shoulders broad, and his muscles rippled under his thin jacket. His moustache drooped like the whiskers of a wet cat. He straightened his string-like tie, tipped his Stetson at an angle, and walked up the driveway to the stoop of the house, his pointed-toe, snakeskin boots looking like weapons that could inflict major damage.

Linda came out to meet him. She was showered and had her long black hair combed back with wildflowers stuck in it. Her white cotton dress fluttered in the wind. I don't think she was wearing any of those under things that she washed regularly and hung on the clothesline. Her perfume—lavender—strongly overpowered the man's scent. I trailed behind him, downwind, not wanting to miss this meeting, yet wanting to stay out of range of those mighty boots.

The wind picked up, and his scent gushed up my snout. Huh! I was immediately taken back to that awful pond. Of course, it was *that scent,* all right. Darn, was I really getting old? How could I warn her that this man was a killer— of dogs? I barked loudly and whined. The man turned and surveyed me. His boots twitched, and I hung back, barking, accusing him of murder. But these humans— what the heck did they understand about us animals?

"Shep—quiet!" Linda shouted. "Git back in the shed!"

That's it—banish me to the sidelines when it's important.

Tommy was returning from putting the chickens in their coop, dusting off feathers and chicken shit. "Come on, Shep," he said, ignoring his mother and the man. "Let's go for a walk." He clipped the leash around me.

I barked all the way over to the gulch. I wanted him to go somewhere else, so I kept tugging at my leash. About ten minutes into our ridiculous stroll, Tommy gave up in exasperation. "What the heck is wrong with you, Shep?"

He loosened his grip, and I pulled him towards Mr. Purdy's property line. When we were at the fence, Tommy got curious. He spread apart the barbed wire so I could step through unhurt. I broke his hold on the leash and ran up the ridge. When I got to the pond's edge, I looked over my shoulder. Tommy was staggering behind, out of breath. "Hey, Shep, slow down—you'll kill me."

I charged in and out of the water several times. I dislodged a potato-sized stone with my teeth and laid it at Tommy's feet. I caught his sleeve and pulled his hand down to the stone several times until he took hold of it. I bumped my head furiously on the stone until an orange haze swam in front of me, like that oil flare. Then I ran in and out of the water several times until the haze cleared. That horrible smell was all over me again. Tommy could not detect it. It was only on my sixth attempt at going in the pond that I saw him inspect the stone in his hand and look at me with a worried frown. Now we could go home!

It was a long walk back. I was very tired. I realized that in human years, I was way into old age, in my 60s, as they count years, as old as Mr. Purdy. Humans have to live through more agony on earth than we do. What I was contemplating doing was going to be a better outcome for all, I figured. My life was less important than theirs. That's also why humans are our masters, though we are more intelligent than them.

When we got home, Linda was on the stoop. The flowers had come out of her hair, and she was drinking from the bottle of whiskey. The man and his car were nowhere to be seen.

Tommy ran up to her. "Mom, I know who killed Buster."

"No one killed Buster," she said dismissively. "He drowned, just like that steer down at Dawson's Creek two weeks ago."

"It was him—Jim. Shep showed me how."

She looked up, face paling. "Jim has suddenly become the biggest punk this side of the Rockies."

"Remember how Shep didn't stop barking from the time Jim arrived?" Tommy persisted.

When she nodded slowly, Tommy quickly told his mother what I had done by the pond.

Linda shook her head slowly when he finished. "Son-of-a-bitch! I wouldn't have believed you earlier today. Now, I'm not surprised."

"Did you break up with him or something?"

"He's a piece of shit. Wouldn't budge on his offer to Mr. Purdy, so I told him I was sleeping alone tonight."

Tommy stifled a smile. "Good for you, Mom."

Linda's face started to crumble. "Oh, what're we gonna do, Tommy? He'll be back. And his offer for this property will be lower. I think I hurt his pride."

"We don't have to sell. This is a free country."

"No way, son. That's what the blurbs say. We are the most self-deluded country on this planet. We are *not* free. Money talks."

"We can get a lawyer."

"Who will also need money."

"I'll shoot Jim with Dad's gun if he comes by again."

"I don't want a son in prison. My father died in one."

"Your dad?"

"Yes—I never told you or your father about that. Dirt-poor Injuns are the ones picked up when there's a crime in the neighbourhood. That's why I was running all the way to Hollywood to make money and get out of the trap." She was sobbing softly.

"Dad left us this property; we can't disappoint him." Tommy stamped his foot on the stoop. "I'll put Shep away for the night."

"No—bring her here." Linda cradled me in her arms, and I felt her tears on my back.

"Oh Shep—sometimes you are almost human," she said. "One of my dead ancestors come back to protect me."

The thought made me recoil. Me, a dead ancestor? How could I have been a silly human? Wait a second... do humans end up as dogs in their next life?

Sobs continued to wrack her, and she held onto me. I was coating her in Buster's dead juices, and she knew it. Maybe she, too, wanted pain to dull her weakness.

"They've brought that damned Middle Eastern war home. It's all about oil." Her words surprised me.

I was more decided on my course of action. And I was glad that I wasn't a human.

I was waiting for Jim the day he next pulled into the yard in his black car. He wore a black leather jacket and was accompanied by another man in a suit and a third guy who looked like he had just stepped out of one of those WWF wrestling matches we watched on TV. This third man exuded the other human scent, the acrid one that I had smelt down by the pond.

Jim stood on the stoop but did not enter the house. Linda was standing inside the door with her dead husband's rifle in hand. She was dressed in her buckskin jacket and faded jeans. And there were no lavender perfume and wild flowers on her today.

Jim smiled. "You think you can scare me away with that? First you sleep with me, and now you try to shoot me?" He turned to his companions and laughed.

"Stay where you are. My house and property are out of bounds to you and your cronies," Linda said, but her voice shook.

"Well—here are the papers. Two hundred and fifty grand, still generous."

The man in the suit pulled out some papers from his briefcase.

"Why has the value dropped?" Linda raised the gun slightly. "Have the oil deposits under this land suddenly shrunk?"

Jim grinned. "You're on tainted property, Linda. The poison from Purdy's pond has spread into the water table, and your springs are compromised. That dog of Purdy's was not the only dead animal found. You know that. There are others—livestock—dying in this drought, rushing into the only remaining waters to cool down and dying in them."

"Or, maybe, you're putting those dead animals into our water holes."

His eyebrow began to twitch. "I'll ignore that comment." Then he took a conciliatory tone. "Word's getting around town about the poisoned ranches. I'm trying to give you a break before matters get out of hand. This is the best my company can offer now."

She took the papers from the man in the suit and flung them at Jim. "Get off my land."

Jim's face flushed. He took a deep breath and forced a smile back on his face. "I don't take 'no' for an answer."

"And I am not running away to L.A. to find myself, either. My place is here. I don't need your money. Now, get out!" The gun was pointed squarely at Jim's chest. Linda's eyes were like a rattler's when it's about to spring.

She was not going to win. Jim would wear her down, like he had done Mr. Purdy. The heavy rifle dipping in her arms said it loudly. My way was better. I looked up at the sun going over the western mountain. I would miss that view, and the walks in the gulch, but I would not miss the pond. And Buster's unborn puppies starting to move in my belly may not see those mountains, either. I hoped that when this was all over, Linda and Mr. Purdy and the other impoverished farmers would get a fair price for the wealth they lived over.

I started my run from the barn end, gathering speed across the front yard. It was like chasing those druggies. I was heavier and sluggish, but had enough momentum when I leapt in the air and grabbed Jim's neck. A flash of panic and a muffled yell came from him before my teeth clamped into his flesh, cutting off air to the brain, splashing blood all over. We crumpled in a heap, and I kept biting and clawing, disfiguring his face, choking him until his hold slackened and his flailing ebbed. He subsided into a gurgle. We police dogs had been trained to kill.

When I tore myself away from him, his blood dripped off my snout, dotting the ground. Tommy was aghast, and the man in the suit was pasted against the car, about to faint. I didn't look back at Jim's body.

I lay down before my mistress, exhausted. Tommy unfroze and reached down to stroke my spattered torso, tears in his eyes. I was prepared for these humans to judge me in the way they found suitable; I had done my duty and had finally taken centre-stage with my Shock and Awe approach.

But then I saw the WWF guy pointing a gun at me, and Linda training her rifle on him—stalemate.

It struck me, too late, that this outcome and its fallout, like the war in Iraq, was not going to be as simple as our encounters in the animal world.

THE SECOND CHANCE

Rocco lurches down the corridor, holding the handrail as the ship groans and sways left, then right. Tonight is rougher than most on the Mediterranean; he has walked this corridor many times on the voyage, unable to sleep, plagued by the time zone shift and by ghosts from the past that assail him the moment he allows his mind to rest. The digital clock in his stateroom flashes the moment he begins dropping off to sleep, jolting him awake. He has wondered if his insomnia is partly due to the results of his last medical test, a test that has prompted this voyage.

A young woman in a short, glittery dress careens towards him, swaying from more than the ship's motion. Glazed eyes stare through mascara-plastered eyelashes. She whispers a muffled "Scusi," bumps him, and passes, leaving him in a wake of perfume, perspiration, and alcohol. The sound of the disco thumps through a doorway.

"Oh, to be young and unthinking again," mutters Rocco as he turns and gazes after the woman who has found her cabin and is fumbling with the passkey. She drops the key and swears, and as she bends to pick it up, the ship lurches, sending her sprawling on all fours across the narrow passageway.

He goes to her rescue. He has always done this—rescue damsels in distress—often to his detriment. They were most vicious when he held elevator doors open for them, a practice he has since given up. He reaches the woman and extends a hand. She accepts it gratefully and pulls herself up—she is strong, and he almost falls on top of her, but his grip on the handrail holds. He pushes the fallen key towards her with his patent leather shoe, and she, still holding onto his hand, reaches down and picks it up. She slides it into the lock upside down and starts cranking the door handle violently.

"Uno momento," he says, reverses the key in the slot, and the door swings opens just as the ship tilts sharply to starboard, dragging them both into her cabin. The vessel rights itself, slamming the cabin door shut behind them.

He is inside an unfamiliar cabin. With a drunk Italian woman! Surely, she must be travelling with a young man closer to her age who will barge in at any moment and kick him out. He tries to retrace his steps and leave, but she is still holding onto him with one hand, the rest of her has fallen across the bed—a single bed!

Now it's his moment to say "Scusi," and make a graceful but quick exit.

"I need another drink," she says, pointing towards the mini-bar, her other hand clutching him like a lifeline.

"You speak English?" Her accent is southern hemisphere: South Africa, Australia, or New Zealand.

"'Strailian." She releases his hand, pulls herself into a sitting position on the bed, and self-consciously pats her hair into place. Then she adjusts her bra straps. "And you?"

"American. Once upon a time from Italy."

"My parents are Italian. This vacation was their bloody idea. Our honeymoon."

His eyes stray back to the single bed.

She catches on. "I switched rooms. He's a jealous maniac." She stands and totters over to the mini-bar.

"Don't you think you've had enough to drink tonight?" This woman intrigues him. She is in her early thirties, curvaceous, blonde—obviously dyed, for her eyelashes are dark—and disappointed.

She pulls out two miniatures. "Join me in a nightcap?"

When he starts to say no, her look turns to pleading.

"Please!"

He senses déjà vu, the wildest off-chance that has brought him on this trip, the chance to re-live a memory rekindling with every minute he spends in this cabin in the proximity of this woman. Is the prayer he has offered in church before setting out on this voyage, a plea for lost youth, about to come true? In a fit of abandon he said, "Lord, if death be the price after experiencing that joy, then let it be."

He sits on the edge of the bed. "I cruised on my honeymoon, forty years ago, when we sailed from Italy to America. The ships were a lot smaller, then. And the Atlantic was rougher than the Mediterranean."

She hands him a glass with scotch in it and perches herself on the writing table, nursing her own drink. She is sobering up in his presence despite the fresh infusion of alcohol.

"Your wife must be wondering where you drifted off to. It's easy to get lost on this rig."

"My wife is dead."

Her eyes widen, but she says nothing. They drink in silence, absorbed in their thoughts.

She lays her glass aside and drops onto the bed beside him. Her perfume is strong, lemony. "Do you have pleasant memories of your honeymoon, forty years ago?"

"Very pleasant. Sitting beside you makes them stronger. I couldn't resist the urge to make love to my wife whenever she was close to me on that voyage."

"Was it the first time for the two of you? The sex?"

"Our first time together, yes. Our parents arranged our marriage. Rosina was from my village in Italy."

"Rosina? Ross... Rosario is also from my parents' hometown. I met him when I visited Italy for the first time last year."

"Did your parents arrange your marriage?"

"Nah. I fell in love. Then I returned to Sydney and sponsored him. I came back to Italy and married him last month. We are supposed to fly to Australia after this cruise, and he will be entering my country for the first time—his... our... new home."

"What happened?"

She punches the single bed. "You mean this?"

He nods.

"He was overwhelmed by the sheer variety of women onboard. He's only used to seeing the same fat, hairy ones in his little town. Yet, he was jealous if I gave a man a second look."

"That's not enough cause for a separation."

"How about walking in and finding your husband screwing a blonde Scandinavian woman in your cabin?"

He sips his drink, exhaling slowly. This is moving too fast. Half an hour ago he was walking that corridor outside, alone, trying to tire himself out to sleep. Now, this...

"Your husband is a fool, if I may say so."

"He said he was just having fun, trying to find out what *real* blonde was, that I was not supposed to take it seriously, and that he still only loved me. I switched cabins after that."

There is a loud banging on the door.

"That'll be him," she says and downs her drink.

Fear clutches his heart. What will the husband think if he is caught drinking with the man's bride inside a locked cabin?

"Don't worry, he'll go away," she says. "He's been trying to get back ever since we split."

"Anna... Rosanna—," a hoarse voice on the other side of the door in plaintive Italian. "Please, open up, my sweet."

"He gets rougher a bit later," she cautions.

Soon there is a kick on the door. "Putana!"

"I told you," she says.

"You should call the reception. Tell them you are being harassed."

"I tried that once, and they said they did not want to interfere in a domestic quarrel."

From outside, "Are you trying to shame me? I hear a man inside with you. Open up!"

Inside the cabin, fear prods his heart again. "I'd better explain myself to him."

"Stay." Her hand on his is insistent. "He will go away." She walks over to the door, and her Italian is fluent for a woman raised abroad. "Ross, you bloody cheat. Look at yourself in the mirror before you call me a whore. You can bang all night until you break your bleeding hand, and the crew takes you away. I am not opening this door. So bugger off!"

"Bitch!"

"Bastard!"

Other voices are heard coming down the corridor: guests returning to their cabins. The banging stops. After the ambient noises have quieted down, a menacing tone layers the voice filtering into the cabin from outside, "I'll be waiting here, all night if I have to, for that asshole who is with you to come out. And when he does, I'll break his neck."

Rocco instinctively reaches for the phone, then puts it down. This is not his cabin; there will be more embarrassing questions. He points her towards the phone. "You *should* call reception."

"I'm going to take a shower instead," she says and unzips her dress. She drops the shimmering black outfit on the bed and stands before him in her bra and thong. She is a buxom woman bursting out of her flimsy underwear. "Do I shock you?" She wears a teasing smile.

He sucks in his breath and drinks in her body, her spoor radiating in this closed space. He takes in every inch of her, the husband standing outside temporarily forgotten. Finally, the words gush out of him, "You delight me. I never thought I would look upon youth and beauty again, unless I paid for it."

"Would you like to make love to me?"

"That would be an impossible dream come true, if it were to happen."

She runs a finger over his face, from cheek to chin.

"I'll be back." She steps into the bathroom and shuts the door.

He is left with a racing heart. This is, indeed, moving too fast. But he is resolved to ride out the journey, wherever it will lead, for it appears to be preordained. His first night with Rosina had gone something like this: the teasing and tempting in a closed cabin until he had been unable to contain himself. Has he really been given a second chance, a repeat performance these many years later? Is God being kind? But there is that maniacal husband outside the door. Perhaps God is playing another of His crude tricks: giving with one hand and slapping with the other.

He recalls the doctor's office, just two weeks ago:

"It's returned. But it's slow-growing, considering your age," the doctor said.

"Will it be painful?"

"We have drugs for that, don't worry."

"I mean the pain of giving up the things you once took for granted."

The doctor rubbed his chin. "You'd better see your priest as well."

Now, in the confines of this cabin, he knows he has to face the man on the other side of the door, eventually. He has never run away from his responsibilities: opening the restaurant upon landing in America, growing it and selling it at a loss when times got tougher, getting a bank teller's job in Little Italy afterwards where he spent the rest of his working life until retirement last year, and then watching Rosina pass away from that wasting illness. He'd faced it all, his limitations mostly, without shirking. And after Rosina died there were no challenges left, no mountains worth climbing, only a disease that they both took turns sharing, and which he is now destined to carry with him to his grave. No more mountains, until now...

She returns, wrapped in a dressing gown, and he knows she is not wearing any clothes underneath. Her hair is damp and silky and curly around the ends. Despite the lack of make-up, she is fresh and beautiful. She pours two more drinks from the mini-bar and hands him one. There is a determined look on her face as she glances towards the cabin door.

"Salut!" She takes a gulp, places the glass on the side table, and opens her dressing gown, giving him a full view of her naked body. He'd guessed right that she was a brunette. She throws her arms around him and kisses him, and he tastes toothpaste, scotch, and the animal breath of lust. Another kick lands on the cabin door from the outside.

He takes her, surprised at his sense of urgency, as if the semi hard-on that has risen inside his pants will drift away like a swiftly receding wave in the ship's wake. Thus begins the slow rhythm of their lovemaking. He is like a drowning man as he plunges into her and back into another time when he entered another wet, pulsing woman for the first time.

"Rosina, Rosina...." he murmurs, and she smiles and thrusts herself up at him, allowing him to enjoy the memory of that other woman. And he doesn't even know this woman's name... is it Anna... or Rosanna? It doesn't matter. To him, she is Rosina, given to him by God on this one night of time-travel. The kicking on the door becomes a drumbeat to their lovemaking, and the rolling cruise ship is a giant water mattress.

When they are done, they lie amidst sweat-soaked sheets, the heat of their bodies evaporating swiftly in the air conditioning. His penis relapses into its habitual slumber, yet twitches occasionally to signal satiation. *Not bad for a guy with a cancer gnawing away at his insides.* The kicking outside has stopped.

"Grazie," she says, running a finger down his chest. He snuggles under her arm, inhaling her youthful essence.

"God was kind to me," he says. "He gave me the second chance I came foolishly looking for on this voyage."

"And He gave me at least one good memory from this cruise."

A feeling of loss hits him in the pit of his stomach. "We are mismatched for each other. I must be older than your father."

"Yes. In another time, we might have been perfect."

"I suppose I should go. He will be still out there."

"You don't have to go. Stay the night. He will eventually get tired and leave, looking for fresh pussy before the casino closes."

It is awfully tempting to stay, to partake of more of the "gift." But he knows he has to pay his taxes. There has never been a free ride, at least not in his life. Taxes and death...

He rises and dresses.

"Will it be painful?" The doctor had never answered his question.

He looks in the mirror and straightens his jacket and tie. He grins wryly; the last mountain has just been climbed. Bending down over the bed on which she is still sprawled, he kisses her on the forehead, mouth, breasts, and dark mound. "Goodnight. Have a good life."

He sees the burly man barring the door when he opens it—short-cut hair, thick moustache and beard, handsome swarthy features. A throttled snarl escapes from that face. *My age must enrage him more.* He sees the hand swinging through the air and feels the smash of the blow that catches the side of his head and sends him crashing against the iron doorframe. He hears the woman inside the cabin scream; she is finally scrambling for the phone. He must allow her to make that call so help will arrive in time, at least for her. He staggers up to block the doorway again, tasting the salty, metallic liquid flowing down his face. *This is a better way than with drugs.*

He feels his knees begin to buckle as the next blow, the killer punch, wends its way through the air. "Thank you, God," he prays before it makes contact. "You are the giver and the *taker* of life."

As he falls to the floor, he realizes that God is, indeed, merciful for answering his prayer and giving him a physical taste of Rosina back in that cabin, before taking him away to meet her in spirit.

THE SUPREME LEADER'S BIG DAY

Arvind, Supreme Leader of Kanjipoor, awoke on a monsoonal morning and looked out of the window at his palatial gardens. Ruffled satin sheets, embroidered curtains, and the fragrance of jasmine flowers surrounded him. A faint whiff of semen and sweat coming off the bed reminded him of the concubine who had visited last night: she had been young, about 16, but old enough to know the moves he liked. He sought them younger these days. He made a mental note to check in with his minister of internal affairs about their continuing supply.

He flexed his muscles, opened the panelled window, and looked outside. The light rain splashed in; warm humid drops that would slake the thirst of the flowerbeds and drive them into a frenzy of renewed growth. He was naked, his limp phallus trailing between his legs. Having an eight-inch penis on a five-foot five-inch body was proof of his virility. Penile length ran in his family, justifying its claim to ruling this small oil-rich nation, but it bothered him that his member did not stand erect for very long anymore. And he was not prepared to take medication for it—at least not yet. He was not supposed to stand in the window, either—snipers, he'd been warned—as his room was the highest point of all the structures in the palace complex. But he was confident the soldiers in the guard towers surrounding the palace perimeter would ward off trouble. He needed to be seen with his manhood exposed occasionally, proof of being the brave leader, unafraid. It was a pity that his son, Abu, did not show the same promise of genital endowment.

The dream he'd had last night was unsettling. In it, the serpent head of the national flag had come loose during a military march-past; the creature had floated through the air, leaving the fabric of the fluttering flag behind, to sting him fatally in front of his citizens. Arvind had woken up screaming and kicked the young concubine out of the bed and out of his chambers. The girl ran away cowering, grabbing what scraps of clothing she could lay her hands on. His return to sleep had been troubled with further nightmares.

Now, Arvind flexed and pulled in his soft stomach, giving up after the third attempt. He was, after all, the Supreme Leader. He would make soft paunches, receding hairlines, and flabby cheeks the latest fashion statement when his new set of public portraits was released next week. He hadn't posed for photographs or paintings in three years. The last ones had been taken soon after his armed campaign against the neighbouring Hawa Islanders had ended; he had been dressed in full military regalia and looked trim and agile. The indolent life of this palace, with no wars in between, had dulled and aged him. Perhaps, he needed another war. He would check for its economic viability when his finance minister visited.

He clapped his hands, and the giant filigreed oaken doors opened. Three uniformed man servants came in, heads bowed; they never made eye contact. In the corridor, two armed guards crossed positions.

One servant helped him into his multi-hued dressing gown and slippers while another opened a side door that led to the royal bath; the third was already mixing the right composition of bath salts and oils into the steaming water. Immersed in foaming, sudsy, fragrant water, with his servants inside the door and ready to pounce and provide service at the flick of his wrist, the Supreme Leader contemplated his day ahead. Today was going to be a special one. His plans for the future would be put into play. There was no sense in delaying further, especially after last night's dream.

The ministers filed into the office located just outside the bedchamber. It was a huge oval room with no windows, and it gave Arvind the sense of a contained world—his world, and he was its master. There were peepholes with shutters at the four cardinal points of the room that offered an unobstructed private view of Kanjipoor.

The lighting was bright on those directly facing the Supreme Leader, while ambient on his side, leaving him in pleasant shadow. He could see the twitch of a face, the flicker of an eyebrow, the tug of a cheek. He could watch for the intake of breath, observe the hunch of shoulders, or the flinch of neck muscles as he issued orders and never accepted advice in return.

Vikram, the minister of finance, was a pale, thin man, losing his hair rapidly, and he had the twitch. He would have to be replaced soon, the Supreme Leader made a mental note. The minister of the interior, Shah, looked smug, and it showed in his paunch; being privy to the Supreme Leader's sexual shenanigans also kept him favoured. Shah would have to be gotten rid of sooner—entitlement is a deadly feeling to keep a minister basking in for too long. As for Chief Minister Salgado—aristocratic, educated but showing the strain of being in the job for five years—he would also have to be replaced before he made a mistake: a man can only go on for so long before he stumbles. Arvind had been carefully grooming their successors over the last few months, unbeknownst to the ministers.

Vikram cleared his throat, his twitch ratcheting up a notch. "We will have difficulty funding another war with the Hawas. We are still paying for the last one."

Arvind narrowed his eyes. "Sell another oilfield to the Americans,"

"The oil price is depressed now, Your Excellency, thanks to the recession in the west."

"Discount the future price to them."

"We can't interfere with the futures markets, Excellency. They are governed by global forces, no?"

"No. You make a private deal, Vikram. How many times have I told you not to think about global forces? Our oil company client will be happy to make a back-room deal. Hah—Shah—what news?"

The minister of the interior bowed his head, a gleeful smile playing on the edges of his mouth. "The president of Nesaram wants to offer you his sixteen-year-old daughter in marriage, Your Excellency."

Arvind smiled, smirking. *Sixteen years—just the right age.* "Nesaram, hah—they have a diamond industry, no?"

"Yes, Excellency. And, Excellency—knowing we have a new regional ally will keep the Hawas in check."

"But that Nesaram president, he is a wily fellow, no? Didn't he and my father have trouble once? When I was at university in America?"

"Ah, that was over a small border dispute, Your Excellency. There was an offshore oil field on both sides. Your father said it belonged to us."

"And by marrying his daughter off to me, he gains access to it and ends the dispute, nah? Is she beautiful, this daughter?"

Shah rubbed his palms together, and his fat lips had saliva at the corners. "Like a cherub, Your Excellency. And a virgin. You can't find too many of them these days, unless you grab them before puberty. She is also very studious and pious."

"Studious? Pious? Then she would not be good in bed. Only good for making babies. And I don't need any more babies."

The Supreme Leader left Shah's evaporating enthusiasm and turned to his chief minister.

"So, what is this I hear that they are planning an internal coup—those Hawa buggers?"

Salgado straightened his back, his long silver mane dancing on the edges of his collar, and looked Arvind directly in the eye. "It is only a rumour, Excellency. It's very difficult to prove. The Hawas are already among our people."

"Then have all the Hawas rounded up and killed."

"That will be a huge task, prone to error. Remember your grandfather's plan to bring in Hawa workers for the oilfields sixty years ago. We all look alike. They have inter-married and integrated very well over the last three generations."

"I don't care. Look through their birth records. Any Hawa blood—get rid of them."

"That is about ten percent of our population. If we make this too overt, we risk UN sanctions and possibly an attack from the Hawa Islanders themselves."

The Supreme Leader looked at his chief minister. *The man has certainly got to go.* "Who the hell advertises what we do to the outside world? No one needs to know. Salgado, are you going to do this job, or do I have to get someone else to do it?"

The chief minister went a shade red under his calm demeanour. "I'll see how we can execute this, Your Excellency," he said, his shoulders sagging.

Arvind waved his hands; the audience was over. As the three men turned to leave, he said, "Oh, Vikram, can you stay behind, please."

When the others had left, Vikram rocked on his heels nervously.

Arvind looked at some papers on his desk, ignoring his minister. After about two minutes, broken only by the shuffling of paper, he looked up. "Salgado's grandson recently married a Hawa woman, no?"

Vikram bowed his head. "Yes, Your Excellency."

"You have to watch that Salgado; I don't trust him. Will you do that for me?"

Vikram looked up, as if searching for a sign to show why he was in favour, grabbing at hope that he was indeed chosen. "Yes, Your Excellency. I will do that."

"Okay, you may go." The Supreme Leader looked down at his papers again.

A few minutes after the minister of finance had left, there was a knock on the door.

"Come in."

Shah hobbled into the room. "There was a summons waiting for me at my office, Your Excellency, saying that you wanted to see me again."

"Yes, I wanted to see you alone. There is something I want you to do for me. That Vikram chap, I think he is embezzling money. He is in cahoots with the oil company. They bought him a villa in the Caribbean recently. He thinks I am ignorant. Follow his movements and report back to me."

"Yes, Your Excellency." Shah rubbed his palms together and bowed.

When Shah had left the room, Arvind picked up his private phone and dialled a number.

"Your Excellency," Salgado answered wearily on the other end.

"I want you to tail Shah. That sixteen-year-old bride story is a lie. I can get plenty of sixteen-year-olds. I had one last night. And virgins too, if I want them. Put a tail on him and report back to me in a week."

"Yes, Excellency." Salgado sighed; this was something he had done frequently in the past.

The Supreme Leader put down the phone and looked satisfied. A good morning's work. His father would have been proud of him.

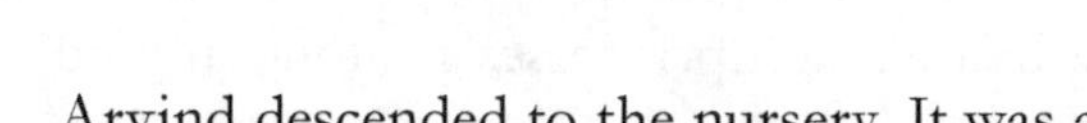

Arvind descended to the nursery. It was a bulletproof glass-domed room about 250 yards in diameter, decorated with elaborate fish tanks and artificial trees and flowers. A toy train ran the perimeter of the room, chugging through miniature waterfalls and tunnels. A profusion of toys strewed the central area. The Supreme Leader made a mental note to stop the weekly supply of new toys from today.

A male child, about six years of age, was rocking on a horse. He jumped off the horse to pick up a toy gun lying on the floor and start shooting at the miniature train that had just passed him. Then he was off to jump on the trampoline in the corner, doing neat cartwheels, shrieking in excitement whenever he executed a manoeuvre, something he had only recently learned. The Supreme Leader made a mental note to send the gymnastics coach a congratulatory letter.

Arvind was disappointed that there were no new additions to the dozen sketches on the sunny side of the room, and the music sheets on the grand piano were strewn carelessly on the floor. The woman, wearing a shawl over her head, hovered constantly in the vicinity, alert to a slip or fall that may occur during the child's rambunctiousness. When she saw Arvind enter, she straightened up and bowed her head. She looked up at him; apart from a tinge of sadness at the edge of her eyes, her features were mainly impassive. Alia, she was still beautiful, Arvind observed. Only twenty-five and the mother of his sole male heir. And how many official wives had he gone through to sire this one child? He couldn't remember. Of late, he had started to give his wives only one chance: if they bore a girl, he had them and the child executed. He had enough princesses running around in the palace already.

"You are leaving with Abu today," he announced.

She looked alarmed, despite his warning her many times in the past that this day would come.

"Why today?" she asked.

"Because I say so." He looked down on her, puffing his chest.

She must have realized, that in addition to being her husband, as the Supreme Leader he was capable of dishing out life or death to the citizens of Kanjipoor, and she bowed her head again. Arvind smiled benignly, although he felt weighted down. This was the hard part. *They think I do not have a heart.* He took out the envelope containing instructions from his pocket, handwritten by himself. He did not want any traitor to make a copy and get it into the wrong hands.

"This will tell you what to do. Memorize it. Then give it back to me before I leave this room."

He walked over to the child. The cherubic eyes of the boy appraised him, then the impish laugh took over and Abu vaulted off the trampoline into his arms, nearly knocking him off his feet.

"Abu, Abu, you have to be careful," Arvind said, stroking the child's dark curls. A film of perspiration from Abu's exertions covered his face, and his clothes were damp.

Arvind straightened out the boy and looked him in the eye. Somewhere deep inside him, he recalled his own father giving him a similar lecture.

"You are going on a long journey with your mother. I will not be joining you for a long time, you understand?"

"The boy pouted his lip. "Why?" His voice was high-pitched. The Supreme Leader hoped that over time Abu would adopt his own husky timbre.

"There are times in one's life when these things must happen."

"But I want to stay here. I have all my toys here."

"You will have toys where you are going, too."

The boy stamped his foot. "But I want to stay right here!"

The Supreme Leader straightened up. There was no point in arguing with a child who got everything he wanted. Thoroughly spoilt, Abu was, but that was necessary for rulers who had to get what they wanted. "Go back to your trampoline. I need to talk to your mother."

He gently pushed the boy back to his pastime. He felt sad that he could not connect with this boy and relive his own lost childhood through him. The child was pre-occupied with material things and did not have any real feelings—good for a ruler, but not for what Arvind had planned for him.

"No, I want to play with my video games now," the boy shouted back and ran to another corner of the room where a game console lay on a table. Very soon, the large video screen in front of it was popping with screeching, squealing, and explosions.

The Supreme Leader stretched his hand out to Alia, and she handed him back the instructions. She had a good memory, and he had no doubt she had digested the salient points. "Hamid and two military units will escort you, Abu, and your maids to the air force base. A squadron of fighter aircraft is standing by to accompany your plane to Sabah."

"I don't need Hamid or his men to come along."

"That is my decision," The Supreme Leader said, his voice rising. *This woman still had spunk in her. She thinks that she has power over me just because she is the mother of my only son. When Abu is older, perhaps Alia needs to be replaced, too.*

"If Abu is troublesome, give him a tranquilizer. I don't want to draw attention to your party."

Her eyes glinted back at him. "I will manage my child."

"Our child," he reminded her.

"Make sure the boy contacts me daily by the secure video link. I want to see him grow up, even though I cannot be with him. And I want him to concentrate on his music and his painting." Arvind felt a lump in his throat and cleared it. He could not show his weakness in front of this woman.

"This boy needs a father—someone he can touch and feel. Not someone who comes in and out of this room infrequently and now will only be at the other end of a video screen."

"He is the son of a ruler. My father was the same way. That is the burden of privilege." The Supreme Leader turned on his heel and stormed out the door. That woman always got to him!

This time, however, he knew his son would not be repeating his own legacy of inheritance. This was too much of a burden to place on one's progeny, as Arvind himself had come to bear. Abu would never be coming back to Kanjipoor but would live a life of ease surrounded by wealth hoarded in Sabah by his father over the years— the self-actualization of the Supreme Leader's endeavours on earth. The boy would grow up to develop the talents Arvind thought he had seen glimpses of in his son: art and music. The child liked thumping the piano, and his sketches of male and female figures actually had proportioned hands and feet, contrasting with Arvind's own attempts as a child when all he could manage was to draw stick people.

The ruler of Sabah depended on Kanjipoor's oil, and binding trade agreements were in place to ensure the pipeline continued, irrespective of regime changes that might occur on either side in the future. Besides, the Supreme Leader knew that even if there was a *coups d'état*, no new Kanjipoor regime could stop exporting oil to Sabah, its close neighbour with a built-in oil supply chain infrastructure integrated with Kanjipoor's. A guaranteed source of perpetual income. But there were days when even these carefully laid plans bothered him. Human beings were such changeable creatures—cutting their noses off to spite their faces, at times.

The visiting delegation from the European Union came to lunch; a terse, polite, and inscrutable bunch trying hard to be cordial. The Supreme Leader was bored throughout the meal and kept yawning during the pre-lunch speeches and toasts. He forgot to take his prepared speech with him and delivered it off the cuff in front of some embarrassed faces. Salgado, sitting next to him, had to remind His Excellency that President Sarkozy was from France, not Belgium, and the present chancellor of Germany was a woman, not a man. How could he keep their constant changes of government in mind? In this country, the ruling family had governed for eighty years—no brainwork involved. He left the meeting early, delegating Salgado to tackle the business matters that were to follow. It was simple: The EU needed Kanjipoor's oil, despite all the flowery speeches. All Salgado had to do was stick to the strict price guidelines laid down by his Supreme Leader.

Arvind decided not to order a concubine during the siesta hour and spent it in the family museum instead. Sex in the afternoon made him sleepy, and recently he had been noticing he could not perform well at night if he indulged during the day. Tonight, he would have the company of the mysterious Rekha; a belly dancer who had arrived in Kanjipoor six months earlier and had opened a dance studio in the capital. Standing six-feet tall with dark hair reaching to her waist, she had a long aquiline nose that narrowed her eyes to a hawk-like gaze. She was lithe with a full body and large breasts he was dying to get lost in. During the first dance she performed at the palace, in front of a large audience of ministers, bureaucrats, defence personnel and foreign dignitaries, she had held his eyes right throughout her show, as if she was dancing only for him. He had commissioned her for special occasions after that, especially during private soirées with visiting business and foreign leaders. He'd never once suggested anything more. Tonight, he had invited her to be his guest at the dinner he was hosting for the EU delegates. She would sit at his right, and he would invite her to his private quarters later.

The family museum was at the eastern end of the palace gardens, a concrete bunker tucked inside an ornate neoclassical facade. It had to be capable of withstanding a nuclear attack, such was Arvind's paranoia. The giant metal doors standing at the entrance of the inner bunker were controlled by computer-generated keys contained in a black pouch held on the person of the Supreme Leader. Duplicate keys were stored in a Swiss bank.

He entered the inner chamber of the museum by activating the doors from his keypad. The cold hit him, and he stifled a shiver. The bodyguards, who always walked within easy reach, stopped at the doors: no one was allowed beyond that point except for the Supreme Leader and Abu, on occasion.

Dim lights flickered along a corridor; the walls on either side were adorned with portraits of the ruling family. Arvind's great grandfather, Abu Bakker, had usurped power in a military coup back in the late 1920s. He had consolidated his power by siring a dozen children, all of whom were given important political portfolios when they grew up. Arvind's grandfather Bazzam, being the eldest, became Supreme Leader, but was infertile having suffered a severe case of syphilis as a teenager. In fact, Bazzam's miraculous escape from death is what confirmed to his siblings that he should rule. After he had run through half a dozen wives, Bazzam recognized *he* was the problem with continuity of rule. Worried about losing the kingdom, he had all his siblings and their children murdered, sparing the life only of his nephew and Arvind's father, Arragon: a strong athletic type who was sure to procreate the next generation. Arvind was shipped off to the best schools in Europe and then to the US for university education and brought back to Kanjipoor only when the ostensibly healthy Arragon was stricken by a mysterious illness—officially termed cancer, but later confirmed as AIDS—and felled very quickly

The portraits on the walls began with the dozen extended families of his grandfather, smug, proud, smiling—taken before they were rounded up one night by Bazzam and sent to the gas chamber. Special religious services were held to recognize their demise, streets were named after them, and these portraits were enshrined in the family museum. The slaughter of the families was recognized by a national holiday, a day intended to strike fear into the hearts of anyone considering dissent.

The corridor led into a series of connected antechambers where the burial vaults of the murdered families were interred. Arvind paid homage to his grand uncles, grand aunts, and their slaughtered siblings, all reposing in a permanent slumber, cleansed of any animosity towards his grandfather whose body lay interred in the central chamber.

Arvind stepped up to his grandfather's tomb, his shoes clacking on the stone floor and echoing off the high walls and oval ceiling. The tomb was made of a shiny red marble with ornate bas-reliefs of the serpent motif Bazzam had adopted as the symbol of Kanjipoor after he had deposed his family and squelched all possible opposition. Over the tomb, a giant tapestry of his great grandfather Abu Baker hovered, his devilish moustache still wrinkling and one eye arched down at his infamous son who had committed fratricide.

Sitting in this giant central chamber, Arvind felt protected by his dead ancestors. There had been coups and invasions against Kanjipoor. The Supreme Leader revered and believed the unbending ruthlessness exhibited by his great grandfather, grandfather, and father had been chiefly responsible for safeguarding the country. Of late, though, he had begun to ask himself if this effort was worthwhile. Surely, enlightenment comes after many generations of doing the same things. At some point one has to ask if this was all there was to life? The Supreme Leader had no doubt he was the creation of his ancestors, but did Abu have to follow the same path? The child did not have the temperament of a future ruler.

The Supreme Leader looked at his great grandfather's tapestry. "Am I doing something wrong? I wear this mantle everyday and keep the subterfuge of treachery alive. No one trusts anyone anymore, and therefore, the kingdom is safe—that is what you taught me. Yet, I can't sleep at night. My son is leaving me today, fleeing this yoke of perpetual terror. Am I doing something wrong? Am I falling apart?"

He was shouting by the time he finished his tirade and was clenching the corners of his grandfather's elevated marble coffin. Great-grandfather Abu Baker just wrinkled his moustache back at him. This was as much as Arvind could expect from them, but it felt good to shout like this; there was no other place to do it without attracting undue attention. There were times when the forces of power and love for his son pulled him apart.

When he stepped out of the metal doors into the antechamber where his guards hovered, the Supreme Leader was back in control, composed and thankful for that bit of therapy.

Across the tiled patio, chaperoned by two matronly women in flowing robes, six girls between the ages of twelve and seven, dressed in the bright oranges and reds of the Khanjipore flag, were shuffling and giggling among themselves. He recognized the older one—Amina—the others he had not paid much attention to, and they had only increased his exasperation as they were born in rapid succession. Coming out of the family museum, he felt a gush of warmth and guilt envelop him when he saw the older girl striding ahead of her sisters, her dark hair trailing behind her. *She will bloom into a beautiful woman soon.*

On impulse, he raised his voice and called out. The group stopped, heads turned, and, except for Amina, immediately bowed, the nursemaids actually falling to their knees. Arvind's oldest daughter looked directly at him and smiled, her dark brown eyes and high cheekbones similar to his. He went up to her and embraced her, something he had not done in a long time, and he felt her young, wiry body yield to him. Feeling embarrassed for this impetuous act in public, with guards in the surrounding watchtowers as witness, he broke loose and held her at arm's length. There was longing in those eyes for the many nights that he had deserted her as a father, relegated her to the care of nursemaids, and focussed his attention on Abu instead. She said nothing but looked into him, making him feel guiltier by the moment.

"How are your studies?" he asked.

"They are well. I am learning Mandarin now."

"In addition to English, French, German and Spanish?"

"Yes."

He was so proud of her, but did not express it. If only Abu was this bright!

"And your sisters?"

"They are well, Father. They are taking music lessons now."

He was at a loss for words. Their conversations had never progressed beyond this point. He took a deep breath. "Good, good. Well, run along then. I mustn't interrupt your study time."

"School is over for the day, Father."

"Oh, yes—I forgot—how quickly time rushes. Well, I have to get off to my meetings. Have a good day, children."

He smiled mechanically and waved them along, left with the searing look that Amina gave him before she took her leave.

The torture chambers resembled hospital emergency rooms: rows of beds under bright lights with equipment positioned around the inmates. The "patients" were strapped to their beds, and the masks on their faces were sometimes used not so much for oxygen as to drown out their screams.

The Supreme Leader picked his way past "doctors" who bowed as he neared and then continued to administer to their charges. The place had to look businesslike and efficient, especially when he arrived and the TV cameras switched on for the "royal tour". Every citizen of Kanjipoor received a daily dose of their monarch walking among those who had betrayed the kingdom; they were entertained and enlightened by their benign monarch walking among his enemies, proud and upright, yet with a compassionate look on his face the camera operators were strictly instructed to capture. *Long live the beloved leader who led with a firm hand and a piteous heart!*

The Supreme Leader approached the bed in the corner, which was bathed in golden glow from warm spotlights. Two white-uniformed men stood by and bowed as he neared. The Supreme Leader paid attention only to the figure on the bed: a body emaciated from all the electroshocks. No one in this facility was marked by bruises—that would not play well in front of the cameras—the torture was inside their bodies. The man had an IV attached to him, and a skull cap over his head to cover where the electrodes had jabbed him. His lower body was covered by a spotless, white sheet; beneath it, the Supreme Leader knew the man's testicles had shrivelled and given out with the radiation he had received—all very clinically done.

The Supreme Leader raised an eyebrow to one of the men standing nearby, and the man nodded. *Good, the microphones are turned off at the bedside.*

"How is he doing?" The Supreme Leader asked.

"Not very well, Your Excellency. He may not last long."

"Leave me with him for a few minutes."

When the men had retreated out of earshot, the Supreme Leader stepped up to the bed and looked down at his former foe: Aqbal from the Hawa Islands, captured in the last invasion that had been quelled by the Kanjiporees.

"You could be spared all this, you know," the Supreme Leader said, turning his pious face towards the cameras.

The man muttered something, but only spittle, tinged with blood, trickled out of the side of his mouth.

"You do not have to be in this prison, you know." The Supreme Leader continued, looking at the cameras, looking concerned.

Out of the corner of his eye, he saw the man hook his finger and raise his head slightly. The last time he had visited Aqbal had been able to speak. The doctors had been expressly warned not to torture the man to the point where he lost his voice. The Supreme Leader leaned closer to the man's face, cautious, in case his old foe jumped up and bit his nose or did something equally desperate. He had turned his back to the cameras.

"You... are the one... in prison." Aqbal's voice was a raspy whisper. The effort of his words was too much, and he slumped back into the bed sheets with a deep sigh.

"You have a child, an heir, spirited away at a young age from your country. Our intelligence has recently uncovered that. How come we did not know that?"

The man's lips parted, revealing that most of his teeth were missing or broken. "You will never find my children. You... will not touch them. You dirty pervert."

"You have no idea of what I can do to you."

"You have already done your damnedest. I am just an empty carcass. I do not wish to live."

"And I can also deny you the right to die by keeping you in this moribund state."

The finger crooked once more, and the Supreme Leader bent further down towards the man's chest. The smell of decaying flesh wafted to his nostrils. *An empty carcass, indeed.*

The Supreme Leader made his last offer. "I'll spare your children. But I want to know who is organizing the coup against me."

The man remained silent, staring up at the ceiling with glassy eyes, and for a moment the Supreme Leader thought he had died.

"Do you hear me, Aqbal? Your men in the other beds will talk soon, even if you don't."

"They will never talk."

The Supreme Leader knew that was true—they were all dead. Lookalikes had been planted in the beds to panic the Hawa leader into talking. Still, Aqbal remained unbending. The Supreme Leader secretly admired and feared his foe. Aqbal did not care for his own life and had a selflessness of spirit that he, Arvind, lacked.

"I am going to increase your dose of electrotherapy, and there will be no tranquilizers afterwards."

"Good, then I will die faster." The voice was fading.

"Oh no, we know how to keep people at the threshold without tipping them over."

The finger crooked again, and the Supreme Leader bent lower, almost brushing the straggly hairs on the man's overgrown moustache, smelling his rancid, pyorrheic breath.

"Fuck off!" The last gasp of the man hit him with a combination of phlegm, making the Supreme Leader spring back, red-faced.

He composed himself, wiped his face with a silk handkerchief, deposited it in a trashcan nearby, and walked over to the two doctors who straightened from their chatting.

"End it, tonight."

The lead doctor raised an eyebrow, and a look of concern spread across his face. "Are you sure, Your Excellency? I think he could be close to talking. They usually talk before they pass, sometimes in delirium. There are drugs we could induce him with."

"No more drugs. Let him die tonight."

The Supreme Leader drew himself to his full height, smiled for the cameras, and strode from the torture chamber.

The reception hall was aglitter, and guests in tuxedos, and evening gowns were gliding about the marble floor, forming and dissolving ad-hoc groups of idle chatter. White-gloved serving staff wove in and out and around the visitors, delicately balancing trays with glasses of champagne and hors d'oeuvres. The women's diamond earrings and tiaras glinted and complemented the giant chandelier in the middle of the room. A sixteen-piece orchestra played waltzes in the background.

The room hushed as the Supreme Leader strode in and paused at the top of the short stairway leading down into the hall. He stuck his jaw out proudly, like his father and grandfather had always done.

Beaming a magnanimous smile, he descended to shake hands with the guests who lined up on either side of his path down the hall. Shah Junior, a young man with a full head of wavy hair and a slow-building paunch—he was the Minister of the Interior's son and slotted for succession, unknown to the minister—grabbed the Supreme Leader's hand in his moist, hot grasp, bowing and smiling.

Oh, if only old Shah had been privy to the private conversations I've had with his son about succession! Junior hated his father for all the beatings he had received as a child, though he was very obedient in the eyes of Shah Senior. The young man had spent hours in the Supreme Leader's private quarters, venting about his cruel father. The Supreme Leader had weaned Shah Junior on some of his concubines and found that he could maintain confidences and keep his affairs private from Shah Senior—good traits for a future Minister of the Interior.

The ambassadors of all the embassies and their fat, old, and snobbish wives were present too, as were the visiting EU delegates, some of them a little bit drunk—they had been through a hard day of negotiations. The ambassador of Nesaram was keen to speak to the Supreme Leader and kept butting in, but Arvind did not wish to be pressed with any more gifts of 16-year old virgins and avoided the man.

The generals of the joint defence forces, along with their junior officers, were also in the room, noticeable in their blue and gold military regalia, used only on formal occasions. They looked particularly alert today, and Arvind noticed none were drinking alcohol. Good, they were respecting the "amber alert" he kept Kanjipoor perennially coloured in.

Vikram was midway down the line, wiping the sweat off his brow—the man never drank, but always sweated and twitched—and bowing shyly. The Supreme Leader missed young Rao, finishing his PhD in America—a perfect replacement for Vikram when the time came. First, he would appoint Rao as Vikram's deputy when the young doctoral candidate returned next year—that should keep his Minister of Finance sweating and twitching even more before his demise.

Salgado was at the end of the line, well starched in his white tuxedo, diamond rings on his fingers, a glass of scotch in his hand, talking to a group of elder citizens who all straightened up upon their Supreme Leader's arrival. Salgado had a distant look on his face, and Arvind worried about that—the man never relaxed, and he never shared what was on his mind. Perhaps when Hamid replaces him one day, a stay at the torture chamber might unlock Salgado's lips.

I hate these people, the Supreme Leader realized. *I have to constantly turn them over to keep this whole system alive.* He looked at the giant painting of his grandfather above the entrance doorway he had just come through and felt that when he next visited the museum he would complain more bitterly than he had done today.

Outwardly, he smiled heartily, accepted a flute of Dom Pérignon, and climbed up on the stage, next to the orchestra, which immediately ceased playing, its members quickly huddling around their instruments to allow him room. The Supreme Leader faced his audience. "Good evening, ladies and gentlemen! To your health and to Kanjipoor's!"

There was a loud cheer and glasses rose, their contents spilled or rushed down already well-oiled throats. The Supreme Leader moved back into the centre of the room where he was surrounded by guests, and he went through mechanical chit-chat, his mind roaming to earlier in the evening when he had attended to Abu and Alia's departure.

The boy had been dressed in a navy-blue suit that he had quickly dishevelled, ripping off his tie because it was "too tight." Alia had a shawl over her head and wore a nondescript beige pantsuit—no make-up—she was still beautiful without it—no jewellery, no perfume. Their bags stood in the hall of the royal quarters, and soldiers were loading them into the armada of vehicles parked outside. Plain clothes bodyguards were coordinating arrangements into crackling radio phones.

Alia looked at him. Her face was puffy and her eyes red; she was going to miss the royal gardens where she had spent most of her spare hours, and the coterie of lady-friends she had spent reading books, having tea, and doing charity work with. A royal wife was always expected to perform these duties, and she had been the perfect, loyal, royal wife. He was going to miss her more than the boy.

"You have never sent us out of Kanjipoor. Is this a wise move?" she asked, pulling the scarf around her.

"Yes, it is for the best. Now is a time of uncertainty. Too many subplots and little cliques are forming."

"But you have created that. Divide and conquer works in reverse, too."

"It worked for my grandfather and father and for many colonial empires throughout history. It is the only way."

"But empires fall in the end."

"Not on my watch."

"Abu will never follow in your footsteps."

"I don't want him to. That is why the two of you are never coming back here." He wished he had not broken the news to her at this point, but felt he owed it to her.

Her eyebrows narrowed. Her intelligent mind was having difficulty with this, he realized.

"Who will rule after me?" he helped her with the obvious question.

She waited.

"After I have cleaned this place of all the plotters, I am going to spend the next twenty years transitioning this state to democracy. No one knows about this yet. I will do it before the Americans and the other westerners try to force it upon us. See what messes they have made in Afghanistan and Iraq. Do you want that happening here?

"When we are seeming to transition of our own volition, that will spark the imagination of the world and neutralize big business and their puppet governments. They will have no excuse to invade us. A despot turning his state into a free country. Gorbachev tried and partially succeeded, yet he is unknown today. No one has *really* done it. I will go down in history for achieving that.

"As for you and Abu, you will live the life you are accustomed to, albeit in a neighbouring state. I will not have my hands tied with you being targets while I am doing my conversion work."

"Why can we not come back once you have rid yourself of the plotters?"

"Because the people will only trust a conversion is taking place when there is no interested heir. Abu will live a life so foreign from this place that he will never want to step into my shoes. You will make sure you turn his attention to other things, to his music and his painting, for example."

In a sudden gesture of tenderness, he pulled her to him and embraced her, not with the lustful urges of his loins but with a surprising unlocking of his heart. He felt her softness and her support. He was definitely going to miss her, but there was no other way.

He strode over to where Abu was operating a fast toy car in the courtyard with a radio console, making a racket over the existing bustle of their departure. He grabbed the boy by his shoulders and swung him around to face him.

Abu's thick lips pouted, one eyebrow drooped: a hidden sadness never allowed to be expressed. Somewhere, the child's subterranean mind was recording all this. But he was still a soft, spoiled kid. His penis did not have the promise of Supreme Leadership. When Arvind had held the baby in his arms soon after the birth, despite his joy at having sired a son, the little, shrivelled, disproportionate rosebud between the baby's legs had distracted him. *Abu will not be subjected to the military training and political apprenticeships my father, just like his father before him, subjected me to. I hope my son doesn't hate me one day.*

Arvind looked down at his son. "Abu, you have to listen to your mother—always. Do you hear?"

The boy looked away, a tear lurked at the corner of his eye. He remained silent.

The Supreme Leader shook him in exasperation. "Do you hear?"

The boy started sobbing, and Arvind let him go and walked away. *He will never be fit for this place. In a way, I am glad that he is going away.*

When he turned back, as he walked across the courtyard towards the office block, he saw Alia draping her arms around the boy, guiding him towards one of the waiting cars.

The sound of the orchestra commencing a vibrant march tune brought him back to the present, and with the loud clash of symbols he saw the person he had missed since his arrival at the reception. Rekha sailed in through the entrance and stood on the upper step until everyone in the room noticed her. She wore a red, body-hugging gown with shimmering gold borders, sleeveless with a deep V-neck that threw out her bosom. Her dark hair was swept into a bun, and her thick gold tiara ended with a cobra's head at its apex. Several matching gold chains of diminishing length, density, and circumference encased her long neck.

The pudgy Minister of the Interior, Shah, appeared from wherever he had been hiding, kissed her hand, and led her down the stairs in the Supreme Leader's direction.

"You look lovely tonight, my dear," Arvind said. He imagined the red dress coming off her body in his chambers later that evening. Perhaps he would keep the gold chains on. *Aqbal's selflessness be damned! Rulers need their dominance—making love to this mysterious woman, conquering her body, would restore that feeling.*

She bowed at him and accepted the champagne flute from the waiter who had magically materialized at her elbow. "To Kanjipoor," she said softly, holding his gaze, a coldness in her eyes that made him uncomfortable. There was still time to melt her and prepare her for bed later.

Shah clapped his hands at the band, and they began the *Emperor's Waltz*, the Supreme Leader's favourite. The guests, as if on cue, made for the corners of the room, leaving a large empty square in the centre.

The Supreme Leader held his hand out to Rekha. She took it firmly, and they stepped out on the floor. As he twirled her, he drank in her essence: a heady perfume mixed with her own bodily musk—it made his head swoon. Yes, he could not be free of this mortal coil that yearned for the pleasures of the flesh. She threw back her head at times during the dance and laughed throatily.

The music picked up, leading to its crescendo as he maintained his hold on her—*the power grip of the leader is exhibited in the dance*—even though her strength threatened to send him off his feet, especially as she was a good head taller than him. The cobra head in her tiara wagged in his face, inches away, tantalizing, tempting and dangerous, just like its wearer; the serpent's tongue was a different colour, like the accumulated poison of a real reptile waiting to spit. He recalled this morning's dream but shrugged it off and tried not to make a false step as their dance quickened.

During breaks between twirls he saw his hapless lieutenants Vikram, Shah, and Salgado in different parts of the room. As the rotations accelerated to the music, he saw the three men drawing closer together and thought it was the pace of the dance shrinking distances. When he went into his final swirl, they all seemed to be standing side by side on the steps of the entranceway, blocking the exit.

The Supreme Leader threw Rekha out of his arms into her final spin, held her by the fingertips of his left hand, and bowed as the music came to an end. He was out of breath, a trickle of sweat pouring down his right temple. Rekha's cleavage glistened with perspiration, but she maintained her mocking poise of superiority.

"Thank you, Your Excellency," she whispered, narrowing her eyes coquettishly and bowing, allowing him one last sight of her heaving, sweaty bosom.

The orchestra clashed symbols, and the Supreme Leader saw the doors in the hall closing. Salgado had exchanged his glass of scotch for a megaphone, and Arvind instinctively reached for the gun in his holster, only to realize that social occasions were the only times he did not go about armed.

"Ladies and Gentlemen," Salgado boomed through the megaphone. "Please stay calm. As of this moment, we, the people, have effected a regime change in this state. Arvind, our Supreme Leader, is no longer in control."

Arvind's cracked, panting protest was drowned out in the flurry of "Oohs" and "Ahhs" and "What the fuck's" that broke out across the hall. His struggle to get across the room was also blocked by the crush of bodies that had surged into the centre at the culmination of *The Emperor Waltz*. The Supreme Leader realized it was the uniformed men who were in his way, on all sides.

"Please stay calm," Salgado announced. "We do not intend to hurt our guests. So, could I ask members of the diplomatic corps, their wives, the visiting EU delegates, and associates to please leave from the right-wing exit doors. Your cars are waiting for you outside." On cue, those doors opened, and the guests started making a mad dash through them.

"Remember, do not try to leave the country, our borders have been temporarily sealed. We will issue new instructions via our media channels shortly."

Abu and Alia—did they get out?

"You don't realize, you idiots," The Supreme Leader managed to cry out. "I have your best interests at heart." His voice was hoarse, and he felt he was losing power by the moment, like the air going out of a balloon.

After the last of the foreign guests had gushed out, the right-wing doors swung shut. Salgado put down his megaphone. The three ministers shook hands with each other.

Mission accomplished—bastards!

Shah Junior walked up to the ministers to take his place on the lower step. His father affectionately put his hand on the young man's shoulder.

The Supreme Leader began yelling louder than he had in the family museum. "You bastard—Salgado! Vikram and Shah—you are in cahoots with him, too? I thought you did not trust him?"

Vikram cleared his throat. He had stopped perspiring. "Your Excellency, it got so complicated after a while, we had to have regular meetings to verify what you had told each of us about the other, so that we did not get our communications back to you all wrong."

Laughter rang through the room.

"My child... Abu... what have you done with my child?"

"Abu and Alia were allowed to leave as planned," Shah, the least confident of the trio, stammered. "The further they are away from here the better. Your daughters will follow them—you had no time for them anyway, Excellency." The fat man grinned nervously and gripped his son's shoulder.

"However, we had to dispose of Hamid," Salgado said. "He had grandiose plans that were quite unsettling."

"I had plans too—for democracy," the Supreme Leader said, looking around at the impassive faces in the room, looking for any sign that someone would believe him.

Behind him, Salgado coughed. "Excuse me, Excellency, history has proven that supreme leaders have difficulty letting go. Whatever democracy a dictator creates is a puppet government still ruled by him. Democracy must come from the people."

"Anddoyouthinkyoucanbringaboutthat?"TheSupreme Leader screamed back at him. "You, who for generations have lived in this... my... totalitarian state? What do *you* know about democracy?"

Salgado looked apologetic. "We have to try, Excellency. Maybe our progeny will get it right, but we have to start the process."

"No one can do it! Look at what they have done in the West. Big corporations will rule you in no time."

Salgado did not answer but hung his head.

"And what happens to me?" The now-deposed Supreme Leader bit his lip as soon as he said the words, but this was important to him, too.

"Leave him to me," said the silken voice behind him.

As the ex-Supreme Leader swung around, he saw a cobra head approaching him; the venom on its tongue suddenly looked real. The face below the snake was hard and fixed, no longer the beautiful alluring Rekha. A darting resemblance to the dying man in the torture chamber flashed before him. *We had been looking for male offspring!*

The last Supreme Leader of Kanjipoor felt his shoulders being grabbed and thrust towards the serpent as it reared its head to strike.

CHATLINE

Once upon a time, when the Internet was new and chat lines proliferated...

She held her breath as the PC powered to life. Would he show up today?

Names were popping up on the side console—Hawkeye, Fat Lips, Sharkey, Lonely Girl, Yogurt. Many others would drop in and out, some to lurk, as the conversation meandered from food to sex to politics to feel-good stuff to alienation to… you name it.

The moderator, Big Daddy, chimed in with his signature: How ya'll doing today?

Yogurt: Slurping on ice cream at the moment.

Sharkey: You never stop eating.

Yogurt: It's better than sex—can't remember when I last had sex. I always remember when I last ate.

Sharkey: The Republicans have pulled out their big money against Kerry.

Hawkeye: Is my Lonely Girl out there?

Yogurt: Sharkey—Kerry's going to lose.

He's been Bushwhacked. Hee hee. This flavour is yum.

Sharkey: You should get out more. I wonder what you weigh.

Private Conversation thread addressed to Hawkeye

Lonely Girl: I'm here.

Fat Lips: Yogurt—try sucking more—it builds your facial muscles.

Yogurt: I weigh okay. My tits are a size D. What's your prick length, Sharkey?

Big Daddy: Hey, folks this is getting a bit steamy. Can some of you take your conversations into your private zones? I don't want to interrupt the flow. Let's stick with the US election string for a while. Sharkey, what's your opinion?

She sat at the computer, most hours of the day, beside her father's picture. In recent times, especially during the past winter, the PC had become her sole conduit to the outside world. The layoff, after twenty-five years with the company, had been jolting, and she did not want to venture outdoors anymore. She understood how Daddy must have felt when the people nearest him had let him down. She had tried to hold onto the few things left: the house and property that were finally debt free and her pension, meagre but sufficient to get by if she did not splurge. The company had been kind and allowed her to buy out her office computer for a token—it was three years old—and she had promptly installed it in her home and splurged on purchasing high-speed Internet access.

The familiar terminal she had logged into every morning was an affirmation that life was still unchanged—her anchor in a fluctuating world.

She was on various chat lines, multi-tasking, impersonating different people she wanted to be. She was alternatively Floozie, Heartless, Femme Fatale, Horny, Loverlot, and many, many more. Alter-egos she knew she possessed but had not been able to indulge in, coming from a strict Catholic family with a dominant mother who went to church three times a week and stopped sleeping with her father the moment the last of the children was born. Her two younger siblings lived in Los Angeles and Paris respectively, and Daddy had died of a heart attack when she was sixteen, but she knew he had really died of a broken heart. Therefore, like Daddy, the pseudonym she liked best was Lonely Girl. Because that was her. As Lonely Girl, she was able to express herself as she really was, without being hurt, like she had been so many times in the past by suitors who had found her "too bland."

The garden lay outside the open window by her desk. When she was not at her PC, she would tend her vegetables. They grew tall and vigorous and tasted masculine. They certainly weren't bland! Perhaps it was all the fertilizer she was feeding them, just as Daddy had taught her. "You've gotta give 'em lots of iron and bone meal and don't forget to water 'em at least once a day, even in the rainy season."

Mother was dead, too, but she'd never cared for Mother and her crucifixes and church meetings. Heck, Mother had spent more time with the parish priest than with Daddy in those final years of his life, letting him drift off like that, lonely and anchorless.

Her job in the tax department at Bowman and Fitch had ended ingloriously last fall, and she was her own person now: free to re-invent herself in any way she wanted. She loved the Internet; it was a better place to flourish than under the gazes of people in public who had always made her nervous and caused her to stammer. One never stammered when typing on the keyboard at eighty words-per-minute. Or when talking to Daddy...

She switched over to her personal online space. Hawkeye was waiting, as she knew he would.

> Lonely Girl: I'm glad you asked for me, Hawkeye.
>
> Hawkeye: Those chat line people are a bunch of morons—self indulgent and passé.
>
> LG: But we met there—that was positive.
>
> H: Yes.
>
> LG: What are you thinking right now?
>
> H: What you would look like... naked.
>
> LG: Oh, you are naughty! That's the boldest you've been so far. I was hoping you would be romantic instead.
>
> H: What *do* you look like naked?

Long pause.

> H: Come on... are you chicken?
>
> LG: Well—my breasts...
>
> H: What about your breasts?

She ran her hands over her flat chest. Nipples poked out at her and froze into little buttons under her touch— that was all she could feel. Men had been disappointed with her breasts.

H: Come on, why are you taking so long? I
   wanna hear about your breasts.
LG: They are a thirty-six D. That big enough
   for you?
H: Yummy… Just my size. Are you blonde
   all over?
LG: Can we change the subject?
H: Wanna go back to art?
LG: You are getting too personal, Hawkeye.
H: Don't you like it? Isn't it time? We've talked
   about art and gardening for too long.
LG: Yes, I like it—but slowly—it's too much,
   too soon.

They chatted about art: his paintings and her poetry. They had one thing in common: death. That's what had been attractive about him. He specialized in painting scenes of horrifying deaths: women being attacked by men, the rape of Rwanda where he had been a freelance reporter. He said that period had entrapped him in a time warp, and he needed to complete many more paintings before he would be free of it. She wrote poetry about death too: how the release of death liberated humans from the toil of living, Daddy being her inspiration. Her best poem was the one she wrote about Daddy dying and being re-born as a wealthy Arabian prince with a harem and women he could make love to at various hours of the day—sometimes multiple times a day—so that he could catch up for the opportunities denied him while living with her mother. The women were grateful for his lovemaking, savouring the pleasure he gave them while sucking his seed into their bodies to bring forth life. She wished she had been able to do the same with her lovers.

They had all been losers. Some were so scared of catching STDs that they double-sheathed, and sometimes triple-sheathed, themselves into shapeless, limp, plastic totems; others couldn't get it up; and others fired off too quickly. Daddy would not have approved of any of them. So, she had remedied things as best as she could and given her suitors something to remember her by. She wondered if Hawkeye would rise above the rest.

> LG: Talking about art is better than sex. It's liberating. That's why I like chatting with you.
>
> H: I prefer sex—it's liberating too.
>
> LG: You are horny today.
>
> H: It's been a long time for me. How about you?
>
> LG: Months.
>
> H: That's way too long! Why don't we get together and fix that?
>
> LG: Not yet.
>
> H: Not yet! It's the third time I've asked.
>
> LG: Not yet.
>
> H: You keep me hanging on so much—it's exciting. Send me a picture of you.
>
> LG: That would break the spell. It wouldn't be a chat line anymore.
>
> H: I'll send you one of mine.
>
> LG: If you like. I have to go now. My vegetable garden needs watering. It's been a rather hot day.
>
> H: Will I meet you on the chat line tomorrow, same time?
>
> LG: Perhaps.

He liked her. She kept him guessing, hanging. Not like the others—the passive ones. He was tired of passive women. He'd had enough of them in Africa. By the dozen. That's when his insatiable appetite for flesh had gone into overdrive. Tribal Hutus would bring their victims over to him, based on what price he offered. Fresh, un-raped Tutsi women, some not older than ten years—that was just after payday. And the tired and bloody older women, when he was running low on cash towards month's end. Africa had been fun, but then, like all places before that, it got too hot for him. When the investigations started, he retreated to safe Canada. Now, he contented himself with "occasional feasts" but was looking for more variety. Lonely Girl was just that, and the Internet was a great hunting ground.

He propped his BlackBerry on the easel and took a swipe at depicting more blood between the woman's legs in his latest portrait. There was always blood after he had finished with them.

The mobile device kept humming and pinged every time a new thread was added to the conversation. Sharkey was dominating the line again with his election bullshit.

He was waiting anxiously for Lonely Girl to join the conversation. She hadn't logged in yesterday, and he had spent two whole hours lurking, occasionally using his Fat Lips pseudonym to tease Yogurt. Yogurt could be another possibility down the road, although she might be big as a house and difficult to dispose of. He wondered if Yogurt was a man in real life—that could be a bigger disappointment—but on the Internet, you took your chances.

He hoped Lonely Girl would join today. The more he dreamed about her, he saw a buxom blonde, fortyish, divorced—she always talked of disappointing relationships—whimsical and arty, yet full of deep unexpressed passion. On the other hand, she could be a lonely unfulfilled housewife.

There she was! Her signature "I'm here" mingling with other threads, and he'd almost missed it. He put down the brush, picked up the mobile device, and went into the adjoining room—his bedroom. He rented in a basement which was partitioned into three spaces: the studio where he worked, a bathroom, and the bedroom housing his "trophies."

He plunked himself on the bed and thumb-typed on the BlackBerry. The hair hanging in plaits on the walls reminded him of past conquests. They were of many colours, strangely, none was blonde. The closest he had come was the auburn-haired secretary he had picked up in a singles bar before going off to Rwanda. Her plait hung just above his dresser. The Rwandan women's crinkly black curls had been difficult to smuggle past Customs, therefore he had no African souvenirs, although he'd had more conquests in that continent than in Canada.

H: You stood me up yesterday.

LG: You don't own my time. That's mine.

H: You have spunk.

LG: I've sent you my picture. Check your
e-mail.

H: I will.

He ran into the studio and snapped on the PC. The picture in his mailbox was striking—blonde, busty, and wanton. More than he had imagined. *What the fuck is she spending her time on a chat line for?* He picked up the BlackBerry again.

    H: That's not you.

    LG: I could say the same of the one you sent
        me yesterday.

He chuckled. He had snipped that picture from a vintage cigarette ad and altered a few features.

    LG: That is me—you can believe it or not.

    H: Why don't I come over and find out?

    LG: Nice try.

    H: We have to meet sometime.

    LG: And then you'll want to have sex
        with me.

    H: Hah, hah—sounds like a plan, doesn't it?

    LG: Have you ever loved anyone?

He started to feel uncomfortable. He rose and paced the room, the BlackBerry sliding into his pocket. He went into the studio and picked up the brush. He splashed colour over the woman's neck, hands, and breasts—bright crimson—that should be more than enough blood. When he fished the BlackBerry out of his pocket, she had logged off. *Bitch!*

She was back online the next day.

    H: I haven't loved anyone.

    LG: Not even parents? Siblings?

    H: Didn't have any. Mother was a prostitute.
        She died of syphilis and related shit when
        I was five.

    LG: Sorry to hear that. People who have
        family are equally lonely, you know.

She is a lonely housewife! He knew it! She'd once told him about her family—father dying of a broken heart, frequenting prostitute dens because he wasn't getting it at home from his frigid wife. It was all bull! *She* wasn't getting it, more likely.

 H: Bet you're not getting it from your hubby!

 LG: Hubby?

 H: You are a married housewife whose husband is fucking someone else.

 LG: And you are a misguided jerk who thinks the way to a woman's heart is through his prick.

He loved this—this woman was powerful, really worth conquering. He went back to his painting, wondering if she would log-off. When he returned a half-hour later, the woman in his portrait was blooming radiantly with blood flowing from every pore of her body. Lonely Girl was still online.

 H: I thought you were pissed off at me?

 LG: I am.

 H: Then why are you hanging around?

 LG: I think we are ready to meet.

 H: That's a change!

 LG: It is—I've just sent you my home address via e-mail.

He was breathless by the time he stumbled over to the PC in the studio and re-opened his mailbox. Sure enough, it was there, and she lived in the next city, just fifty miles away. She could have been in Inuktitut for all he knew.

 H: You still there? You're not far from me— that's a coincidence.

LG: I read all the reports on Rwanda. It was not difficult to spot you and track you down.

H: What do you know about me?

LG: Thatyougotoutofthereveryquicklybeforeit was over.

He started to panic. This woman was smart. What else did she know about him?

H: When you see people dying around you all the time it makes you kind of sick to your stomach.

LG: I know the feeling. You sometimes want to join in, no?

H: How the hell would you know? You sit in your fucking middle-class home and write e-mails every day. And your husband is not fucking you—that's all you know.

LG: You are getting touchy. Come over at eight p.m. on Saturday.

H: And your husband will not be at home?

LG: I will be alone.

He went back into his room and pulled out the box. The knife gleamed in his hand. Time to put it to use again. Besides, she knew too much about him anyway. This one would be easy.

She put the watering can away in the shed. The vegetable patch looked radiant in the dying sunlight, even in these long summer days. The corn would be ripe for plucking in a month. The garden stretched for three acres at the back;

it was so large that she'd had Daddy's remains exhumed and moved to this family homestead after her mother died. She'd built him a custom grave on the property. The siblings in Paris and Los Angeles complained, but as they did not live here anymore she won out on the decision. Besides, they knew how close she was to Daddy. His grave stood on a hill on the southern perimeter looking down on the vegetable patch and the house.

She ascended the incline and knelt by the headstone. She came here frequently. Daddy was the only one she could talk to when she was not online.

"He's like the rest, Daddy. Sorry, I failed again."

The marble stone stared blankly back at her. Dried flowers swirled about it as a gust of wind whooshed by.

"And he doesn't take anything I say seriously. He doesn't believe in the real me. He gets excited only when I talk tough and dirty with him. That's why I sent him the picture of that woman from the travel commercial."

Silence. Except for the swirling wind making her feel that Daddy was sympathizing.

"This one is strange, too," she carried on. "I think he could be dangerous. Better keep a sharper eye on him."

She thought she saw the headstone nod. Daddy was responsive even in death.

"It's a shame there isn't a good man like you out there for me." She zipped up her jacket. "I have to go now. He will arrive soon. Goodnight, Daddy!"

She went indoors, changed into a tee shirt and shorts, and sat down at her PC to check on the chat line. Sharkey was not on yet, and the conversation was predictably a bit slack. Yogurt came on with a new recipe for cheesecake; Fat Lips began asking questions about the ingredients.

Then, to her surprise, Hawkeye appeared online. She moved into the private space to talk to him alone.

> H: I'm on my way.
>
> LG: I thought you would be traveling at about this time instead of chatting?
>
> H: Yes. Plus, I have my cell phone. Are you wearing the slinky black underwear you promised?
>
> LG: And the scent of wildflowers in my hair.

At least that bit was true. She had crushed fresh wildflowers into her hair from the patch that ran free in the uncultivated part of her garden. But her underwear was old and soiled—she'd been wearing them since yesterday, and it had been hot outside in the garden today. Her underarms smelled stale and strong, but she wouldn't be needing deodorant for the work at hand tonight.

> H: I can't wait to get over. Are you excited?
>
> LG: Yes.
>
> H: Do you do anal?
>
> LG: There you go again. It's all about sex with you.
>
> H: It makes the world go round.
>
> LG: For you, it does. Did you follow the rules I laid down?
>
> H: Absolutely. No one in town saw me get on the bus. And I got off two blocks away from your house. I am respecting your privacy.
>
> LG: Good.
>
> H: I'm closer than you think—I'm actually entering your driveway now.

She heard the doorbell ring and sighed. She kept the PC running; there were other tasks to be attended to, other conversations to carry on, later. She went to the door, reaching behind for the baseball bat hiding in its regular nook—Daddy's, with which he'd taught her how to bat in the ladies' little league, those many years ago.

Opening the door with the bat concealed behind her back, she saw a middle-aged, bespectacled, hunched, fat man with a weak smile that was fast disappearing as he tried to reconcile her with the picture she had sent him. He was tucking a mobile device into his jacket.

"H-Haw-Hawkeye?"

"Lonely Girl?"

"Come in!"

Big Daddy opened the chat line.

> Big Daddy: My friends, how y'all doing today? Who's out there?

> Sharkey: I'm here. I told you Kerry's gonna win. He's ahead in the polls. Where's Yogurt? You owe me money, honey.

> Yogurt: I owe you dick. The election's not over yet—you just wait, man. Our George is going to whip his ass.

> Big Daddy: Friends, we have an announcement to make. We have experienced a dramatic drop in membership this week—Lonely Girl, Hawkeye, Fat Lips and a few others—they've all dropped out permanently. I got this bad news for you. Sharkey and Yogurt—you are the

only regulars left. As our hosting costs are getting too much per user, we will be cancelling this chat line as of today.

Sharkey: No brother! Don't do that!

Yogurt: And I was just beginning to like that political asshole Sharkey!

Big Daddy: Well, you two can always join another chat line. Okay, okay, I know we could go on forever, protesting. So I'm going to close this discussion off now—okay? See you folks on another chat line sometime soon. Bye for now!

She started logging off the various browser windows. Sharkey—poof! He had been the hardest to maintain: she'd had to read the political news daily just to keep up with his character. Yogurt was easy, although she could never eat like her. Finally, she logged off Big Daddy. Good. That was the way to bring closure to this episode. Next month, she would open another chat line with a raft of new characters from her imagination.

She looked out over at the vegetable patch where a new plot stood, freshly dug; she'd planted lettuce in it, hoping some leaves would peep through before the frost came. She was glad she had clubbed Hawkeye the moment he stepped over the threshold; he would have been too heavy for her if they had gotten into a struggle. Later, when she dragged his body out, the stiletto had fallen out of his pocket. "I told you this one needed a special eye," she told Daddy's headstone.

Daddy would keep a good watch over them—over all of them who reposed under the vegetable patch. Daddy—the patron saint of loser men—whose beautiful heart beat out there in some other man she was desperate to find, so that she—unlike her mother—could nurture him to his true potential.

"Perhaps, the next chat line will bring me someone worthy of you, Daddy," she said, looking at the picture on her desk.

WHERE THE SUN DANCED
A MILLION FIREFLIES

The man called Ben paced the narrow room. Soon they would come to him, to offer him a chance of support, a court-appointed lawyer. He did not trust these offers. He had only trusted in himself, but now that trust was called into question after what had happened. He felt the shackles that hobbled him and wondered how he would get these people to believe him.

Where to begin?

Where to begin?

The island? Where the surf pounded the shore, sometimes in anger like his father, sometimes in boredom like the neighbourhood kids kicking soccer balls and looking across the water for bigger and better—where the sun danced a million fireflies on indigo waters— where men hung around unemployed, scrounging a few dollars from gullible tourists only to lose them in bars that doled out cheap rum to feed a thousand unfulfilled dreams. The island, where his father had worked at the coconut factory all his life only to see it go bankrupt with mismanagement, evaporating pensions, and throwing men back into those very bars to drown their sorrows.

Ben would dodge school, run down to Smuggler's Bay, and give visitors tours around the town for a couple of dollars. During the school break, he would cut sugar cane and bananas for the estate proprietor who owned all the land on the island. Wielding a machete gave power to a ten-year-old, the only time he was allowed one. The work was hot and back-breaking, and he managed to siphon off a few dollars that he did not have to turn over to his mother at the end of the day. Those were happier times, when looked back upon now.

But home at the end of the day had been a depressing place to return to, where his unemployed and broken father would stagger in and whip the children at random. There were eight kids in the family and "one in de oven" as his mother said. Ben was the fourth in line, the invisible one, the one no one had the time for, the one who had to make it on his own wits. He often found himself under the bed in the single bedroom of the house reading a book, just to escape his father's tirades.

He came out from under that cover prematurely only once: the time when his drunken father bundled in his older sister, Matilda, threw her down on the bed, and started to rape her. A strapping thirteen-year old at the time, Ben grabbed his father's cat-o-nine-tails that hung over the door, an instrument that was used on the children often, and beat his old man to a pulp. He remembered Matilda's screams, imploring him to stop, his mother warbling in from the cook-house holding her swollen belly, and his father's blood-sodden face and sorry sobs which would soon turn to homicidal rage. Ben dropped the whip and ran and never returned home.

He ran down to the harbour and hid on a friend's boat. The next morning, the friend's understanding father sailed him over to neighbouring St. Vincent, where Ben went to the Benedictine monastery to seek refuge. A visiting Canadian missionary took pity and arranged for him to go to Montreal.

No, this lawyer would not be interested in his life with the Benedictines, where he'd had to confess his sins every day and live a cloistered life. The Brothers pressured him to pursue ordination but their claustrophobic regimen was not for him, even though it had given him a firm understanding of right and wrong, and he realized the punishment he had meted out to his father was wrong. "Vengeance is mine," said the Lord, and Ben accepted it, although he wrestled with the concept, just as he wrestled with those carnal desires that were taking over his eighteen-year-old body. When he reached high school, he decided he was going to get out and seek his fortune in the wider world.

Living in Montreal afterwards, working in bars as a bouncer—the only work he could get—sleeping in rat-infested rooming houses, taking comfort from greedy white women who sought the novelty of "big black cock," and living among the dregs of society who reminded him of his drunken father was no life, either. He realized he was a black man in a white man's country, and those generous tourists who had come to his shores long ago weren't as accommodating on their own turf. After ten years of trying to climb the mountain in the city built around one, he quit and took the VIA Rail to Toronto.

He met Claire onboard that train. She was from the neighbouring island of Grenada, finishing a degree in the social sciences at York, hoping to become a social worker back home.

"You could do better," he argued, while his heart melted under her sultry and intelligent beauty.

"We got to stop the desperation," she would reply. "There is desperation in this country, too, just not so much as back home."

"Worse," he countered.

When Claire got pregnant—what could he do, he barely touched her and she started sprouting a baby— she put her plans to return to Grenada on hold. They got an apartment in Regent Park. The rent was cheap, and so was life, but Claire got a chance to practice her social worker skills among the drug addicts and derelicts in the neighbourhood. Ben found a job as a security guard in the suburban bank; a place he worked in until the day of the "event" that landed him in jail. Working that dead-end job, he began to understand his father more—stay put, find security among the madness outside. The Benedictines were seeking it behind the walls of their cloister. The bars here were all controlled by a mafia that offered him no break. At least this bank was not going to go bankrupt like the coconut factory.

He disliked his day job, but more than that, he disliked the wealthy people who came into his branch. They wore expensive clothes and deposited large sums of money but were always quarrelling with the bank staff. They seemed to be unhappy despite their wealth. When Claire's confinement neared, he asked to be transferred to night duty, when he wouldn't have to encounter customers, and where he remained for the rest of his employment.

Those were also happy days: the first two years of Winston's life. Ben fed and looked after the boy during the day while Claire worked at the shelter for battered women; she took over Winston's care at night. Remembering playing in the park with the drooling toddler brought tears to Ben's eyes. They would spend the whole day there in the summertime.

All that changed the evening Claire was returning from work and that asshole of a crack addict went wild and started blasting away with his handgun in the middle of the street. Claire took a bullet in the head and died instantaneously.

Start the story with the raising of Winston? Nah, this lawyer's job was to save the living. Winston had been a handful after his mother's death. It was as if the child developed a grudge against society. An angry, slightly-built boy, bullied and getting into scrapes at school, and getting suspended many times. In desperation, Ben would strap Winston, although he had sworn never to become like his own father. That was the only punishment he knew. As the boy got bigger, Ben had to stop, lest the punishment be visited back on him. Ben began to understand his father even more.

When Winston started peddling drugs around the neighbourhood and writing rap songs, Ben was crushed. He started yelling at the lad, but Winston only turned up the music on his new stereo set. When Winston buried himself in his music, no one could enter his world or his brain, and Ben feared those moments when he lost contact. This newfound wealth was never visible, for Winston kept spending his ill-gotten gains on partying and trying to create the next best hip-hop album that would put him in the leagues of Jay-Z, Drake, and all those other lottery winners. One thing he handed his son, Winston had never got caught by the cops, despite having many narrow shaves, and he hadn't attracted the random bullet that had felled his mother. Ben guessed his son was playing at the retail level, small fry; it was the wholesale guys who wielded the big iron.

When sixteen-year-old Winston got his class-mate, Priscilla, who lived in the next street, pregnant, and she decided to have the baby, Ben sprang into action. He opened an RESP at the bank for the little girl, Cleopatra, depositing ten dollars per paycheque and hoping it would grow into a sizeable sum to help with her university education. When the doctor diagnosed a small prostate problem in Ben that could only worsen over the years, he designated Cleo as the beneficiary of his pension.

Better start here, he thought. Otherwise, there will be no story left...

Ben brought Winston his morning cup of tea at 7.30 a.m.—a ritual he performed daily when he returned from his nightshift and before he went to bed. Winston, nearing thirty and still light years away from hip-hop stardom, lived with his father in the old flat in Regent Park. This suited Ben, for he got to see the teenaged Cleo who lived with her mother on the next block. Winston and Priscilla had never lived together; they couldn't afford it. So, they lived with their respective parents and bounced Cleo between them, fighting like mad when the child was not around. Recently, they had been fighting even in her presence.

"Yo—get up. Time to go to work." Ben placed the steaming cup on the grimy bedside table. He had to move a hash pipe and scattered ashes out of the way. He wrinkled his nose at the after-smell—never could get used to it. At least the house was quiet and not pulsing to a hip-hop beat. Ben shook the sleeping man. Winston had just got a job at a retail electronics store, one of many he had held and lost over the last decade, and he must not be late for work.

Winston yawned and rubbed his eyes, rose halfway, and fell back, pulling the duvet over his head. "Go away, old man," oozed from under the musty blanket.

"Your job, Win. Wake up."

"No need for work. Bitch has taken Cleo and fucked off."

A stone sank down Ben's stomach. Gone? His precious grand-daughter? "Where."

"Back home. To her brother—the bigshot tourist guy in Jamaica."

"You not going to try and bring dem back?"

"Brother will shoot my ass off. He told me last time he was over here. They're gone."

Secretly, Ben was pleased. He'd never had much confidence in Winston ever being a stable breadwinner. Cleo would be safer in the streets of Montego Bay than in this crummy neighbourhood, especially with a father dealing drugs on the side. He was going to miss his Cleo.

"You still gotta work. Hold down a decent job."

Winston got up and reached for his tea. "That's for old guys like you. I'm for the big hit."

"Yeah—Wot's dat? Drugs? Your still living wit your father, dat's de reality."

Winston reached over to his stereo on the other side of the bed and switched it on. The room swelled to a beat that set Ben's heart pulsing synchronously. "Music, can't you hear it? Me and Elroy are cutting a new disc. YouTube and all."

"How many times you done dat? Four... five times?"

"We were ahead of the curve those times. This time we're smack on. I'll show that bitch she left too early."

Ben walked over to the window. Children were walking to school, bundled up for the snow had fallen; Cleo would have been among them, but not today. Not anymore. The neighbourhood felt empty, like when Claire had died. Ben would make sure to wake up from his daytime nap to go down to meet Cleo after school and walk with her in the park, the same one he had taken her father to when Winston was a toddler. Those moments were the highlights of his day. Now they were gone. He took a deep breath and shook off the depression that was descending. He would have to get her address in Jamaica and write to her, tell her about the RESP. It was to have been her surprise when she finished high school.

"You wanna get rich too fast," he said turning away from the window.

Winston shot back, raising his voice over the music. "You've worked your whole life for what? Peanuts."

That was true. His pension was probably not more than fifty thousand dollars.

"At least I put money away for your daughter's education. It's her only way out."

"There's educated assholes selling drugs."

True. There were security guards with university degrees. Still, it was good to hope.

"Don't know where I went wrong with you." Ben took the empty teacup to the kitchenette and washed it. "You should have had a mother." These were the moments when Ben regretted not having re-married, but how could you predict success with a kid as unpredictable as Winston?

"And you tried to be one and failed." Winston lit a cigarette. "You could be better off robbing that bank you work for."

Ben walked away, hurt from this familiar refrain that ended all discussions: "You could be better off robbing the bank you work for." Winston had pipe dreams, like building a recording studio back on the island, a place the lad had never lived, let alone visited. How could he be so stupid? Winston talked as if he belonged on the island, while Ben had run away from there. A kid born in Toronto feeling he belonged elsewhere was sad.

"You always know how you gonna spend de money. But you don't put de effort to earn it. How I gonna rob de bank?"

At which point, Winston would back out saying, "I'm working on it." And he never did. Just talk—like everything else he dreamed about.

Last year, after one such argument, and on an impulse, Ben *had* worked out how to rob his bank. There were two passwords to the vault, one held by his alcoholic branch manager, Mr. Jessop, and the other by Chalmers, the head cashier, another closet drunk. The passwords were refreshed on the first day of each month, but Chalmers, who was nearing retirement, was too lazy to remember his, and had just kept changing only the last two digits in the previous password to resemble the new month of the year, the first six digits being his first name. Therefore, in November, the password would be "albert11," in December "albert12" and so on. Ben had overheard a drunken Chalmers talking about his "password system" at the last office Christmas party. Jessop, on the other hand, had a poor memory and entered all his passwords in a little black book he kept locked in the bottom drawer of his desk, along with a hipflask that got used most afternoons. Ben had come across the black book when, out of curiosity and boredom on one of his nightly rounds, he had wandered into Jessop's darkened office and gone searching for the secret bar that rendered the boss inebriated at the end of each working day.

Armed with both passwords, Ben decided to test his theory on the night he was scheduled to work with Sothi, another guard who slept during most of the night shift. Sothi was in his fifties, had been a refugee from Sri Lanka, and worked three jobs. He used this one to get his beauty sleep. Ben believed the bank had hired Sothi only to boost its employment diversity ratio. Sothi did his customary hourly patrols from 8 p.m. till 11 p.m. then slept in the control room, leaving Ben to handle the graveyard patrols before rising promptly at 5 a.m. to do the last one before they clocked off duty. Given the man's background and struggle to put his three children through university, Ben allowed Sothi his sleep and never reported him to management.

At 2 a.m. on that first night a year ago, when Sothi was snoring his head off, Ben began his hourly walk-around. He paused the camera overlooking the vault, and using the passwords, got inside the steel chamber in less than a minute. He was shocked at his own audacity as he stared at the insides of the vault with its neat rows of banknotes, traveller's cheques, and other financial papers. A feeling of power surged through him. No longer was he a tadpole in the hierarchy of the universe; he could, if he wished, take this money and ride off into the sunset. He stepped back out of the vault, relocked the door, and un-paused the camera. The whole exercise had lasted three minutes, but it was the most powerful stimulant he had had in a long time. He reported no incidents that night, so the tapes were recycled, and no one knew what had transpired, least of all Sothi who was still in slumber when Ben returned from his walk-a-round.

This three-minute routine became a monthly exercise, each time the passwords were refreshed. Ben started to feel more in control of his life, and the act erased whatever hurt that sprang up whenever Winston goaded him to rob the bank. Yet, respect for the law that the Benedictines had imbued in him had prevented him, thus far, from making it more than a fire drill each time.

Winston did not go to work that day but mooned about the apartment with his music blaring, which made it difficult for Ben to get a proper rest in the adjoining room. Finally, a neighbour from upstairs started pounding on the ceiling.

"Fuck off, you motherfucker!" Winston shouted back and continued rapping to his music. "After tonight, I'm done with you niggers."

Ben rubbed his eyes and sat up in his cot. "What's going down tonight?" he asked.

"Something sweet," was all he got as a reply. Finally, pulling a pillow over his head, Ben tried to get some shut eye.

The house was quiet when Ben awoke at 6 p.m. for his night shift on the first of December. Winston had gone out—strange—the lad never left until way after 10 p.m. and only returned in the early hours of the morning. A sense of gloom enveloped him. He would not be seeing Cleo anymore; that's why he had overslept, dreaming of her instead. He sighed as he put on his blue tie. All his life he had craved stability, and yet Winston always trod risky paths. The young have it hard these days, he figured. *But so did we. We cannot talk to each other. That's the problem! Generation gap, they call it.* He realized today the passwords changed at the bank—those three minutes of buzz would be nice to look forward to, to offset the negativity of the day.

On his 2 a.m. patrol, with Sothi safely snoring in the control room, Ben used the skeleton key to open Jessop's drawer and pull out the black book. The new password was written inside; he memorized it. He wished he could take a swig from the hipflask for he needed a boost today, but he hated alcohol for it reminded him too much of his father. As he was replacing the book, he saw a manila folder. This was the first time he had seen any other contents inside this particular drawer. Curiosity overcame him, and he withdrew the folder. Using his flashlight, he read through the papers, his chest tightening and his heart sinking as he proceeded.

They were being let go! The cover memo, more like speaking notes, written by Jessop, talked about the need for revitalization; the security team had been with the bank for too long, was aging, and had lost its edge; security operations was not the bank's core business; it was time to outsource the function to a security firm.

Hadn't Jessop and Chalmers also lost their edge long ago? Shouldn't they be part of the packaging out? The memo was followed by letters dated the third of December, addressed to each member of the security staff, offering salary continuation based on tenure and age, and access to their portable pensions. Ben's and Sothi's letters were among the pile.

Rage welled inside him, and he had to hold onto the desk. "You work your whole life for what? Peanuts!" rang in his ears. *After tomorrow, it wouldn't matter how many passwords I have!*

He hurried down to the vault. The camera would be on pause for longer than three minutes, but it didn't matter anymore. He was inside the steel door in a few seconds. Using the canvas bags that were piled in the corner of the vault for when the Brinks truck arrived, he stuffed them with cash, taking the smaller bills that would be harder to trace. *There must have been over five hundred grand in there.* He had no qualms about relieving those unhappy customers of their money—they would continue to remain unhappy anyway. The money would enable a fresh start for him and Winston. His parents were long dead, and most of his siblings were scattered around the world. Matilda was still on the island with her many children and grandchildren who were all in the tourist business running taxis, boats, and working in hotels; Ben wasn't sure if they were his nieces and nephews or siblings, given his father's deviant past behaviour. Matilda would look after him and Winston.

He had two bags full, and that was as much as he could haul. He came out of the vault and switched the camera back on. How was he going to get the money out? He had no car, and only Winston had a driving license. He pulled out two garbage bags from a supply cupboard and stuffed the money bags into them, stuck two pink anti-cancer ribbons that were lying on someone's desk on each garbage bag, and ran the bags over to the back entrance where he piled them with the rest of the day's refuse. They would remain there until the municipal truck came at 6 a.m. Snow had begun to fall, and he hoped the bags would not be covered and their pink ribbons obscured.

He went back to the command centre and shook Sothi awake.

"Have to go to de all-night pharmacy. My stomach not good. Everything okay on de patrol."

"Okay, okay," Sothi replied and went back to sleep.

Ben walked two blocks to the bank of telephones, cursing the mounting snow that revealed his footprints like an accusing finger. He'd never owned a cell phone. From a payphone, he called Winston's cell, hoping the boy would still be up and coherent and not stoned in some dive. He had no one else to call. Winston answered at once, catching Ben off guard.

"Win!" Ben paused, a surge of pride mixing in with his mounting panic. He had to savour this moment, when he would get his own back on his son.

"What's up, old man? I'm busy. Big job underway."

"I robbed de bank."

Silence at the other end. Then, "What!"

"Yeah, you were right. I was going to end up with peanuts. So, I decided to be a King Coconut. We rich, Win."

"Shit!"

Ben quickly told Winston what he wanted.

Winston cut him off mid-sentence. "But I can't rent a zip car. My credit card's no good."

"Shit! But de garbage trucks get here at six. What we gonna do?"

Winston was sounding awfully cocky and confident and grown-up for a change. "Leave it to me, old man. You go back to your post, and I'll take care of it. Pink ribbons on the bags, next to the dumpster, eh?

"Yeah."

"Bye, old man."

"You're a good boy, Win. Remember, before six."

Winston had already hung up.

He was impatient to get off duty, but he had to go through the motions for the next three hours. When he got home the snowfall had ended, but there was ten centimetres of the white stuff on the ground, and the streets were a mess. The apartment was also in a mess.

The two pink-ribboned garbage bags lay in the middle of the living room, traces of snow evident in the damp puddles on the linoleum. The bags were open and notes lay in bundles beside them—Winston had been checking out his father's claim. There was also a stainless-steel suitcase next to the bags, unopened.

Winston was on the phone, pacing back and forth, barking orders, losing his cool, and swearing at times. Suddenly, Ben realized how much out of his league he was at the present, although his son seemed to be in control... well, almost. Had he underestimated Winston all along?

Ben had entered a dream the moment he had seen that file folder in Jessop's drawer, and there was no getting out.

Winston clicked off the phone and barked, "We leave in half an hour. Pack some clothes."

"Where we going?"

"Montreal. One of our supply truckers is giving us a ride there."

Bad memories of Montreal returned: of bars and loose women and being a black man with a cock for hire.

"De cops will catch us in Montreal—we stick out. You don't speak French."

"We are only holing up there until a tanker arrives. It will take us out to Trinidad. En-route it stops off at the island. It was arranged for *my* big job."

"How much de transport cost?"

"Lots. We have my money, too. Much more than you made." Winston pointed triumphantly at the steel suitcase.

"Dat your big job?"

"Yeah. Elroy and I pulled a big sale tonight."

"Elroy in dis too?"

"Yeah. I used his car to haul your garbage bags here."

"He knows? Where he now?"

Winston ignored the question and began stuffing the loose notes back into the garbage bags. "Get packed."

Ben staggered into his bedroom, pulled out his old suitcase from under his bed, the one he'd come to Toronto from Montreal with thirty years ago, and started tossing a few clothes inside. He made sure to pack the family pictures: Claire in her social worker's uniform, the same one she later died in, little Winston in the park in his stroller, Cleo on her first day of school, and another when she received her first holy communion. He paused over the photographs—happy times, even though they had not felt so at the time. Far better than where he was now.

When he emerged from his room, Winston shoved something at him. "Here, for your protection. Use it if you have to."

Ben felt the oily steel in his hands and his dismay deepened. "So, now you playing in de big iron stakes?"

Winston hefted the steel suitcase, a look of pride on his face. "When you play in this league, you need protection." He grabbed the two garbage bags in his other hand and hauled everything to the front door. "Let's go."

Winston was highly agitated, like when he was on one those uppers he took that kept him on the move all the time. He appeared to be scared of their reality and looked like he was trying to stay ahead of the fear. In a daze, Ben tucked the pistol into his waistband and followed, locking the front door behind him, knowing he would not be returning to the home that had been his for half his life. This had all gone horribly wrong.

In the basement parking garage, Ben recognized Elroy's Honda Civic with its garish neon green windscreen border, parked in a visitor spot.

"Where Elroy?" he asked.

Winston ignored the question and stuffed the money bags in the back seat.

"Open de trunk." Ben said. "Back seat's full."

"Trunk's full too. Pile your suitcase on top of the bags in the back." When Ben hesitated, Winston grabbed the old suitcase from his father and crammed it into the rear seat.

"Okay, we gotta go."

"Where Elroy?"

"He let me use his car. He will join us on the island. He arranged the trucker and the tanker. It's all under control."

Winston pulled out of the parking garage, steered slowly through a few snow-clogged streets, and hit the Don Valley parkway. The tiny car strained at first, overloaded, but it picked up better on the higher gears. The inside smelled of rotting meat.

"Why we need a trucker? You could drive dis car all de way to Montreal."

"Car's hot and looks like a circus. We'll be lucky to get to the truck stop in Bowmanville. That's where we're being picked up."

"You were going to produce a DVD with Elroy. Now you driving his car and all dis money."

"My bad. I didn't want to panic you."

Ben sank back in his seat. The smell in the car was nauseating. He opened the window a crack, but he could not relax. The pistol dug into his side. He pulled it out of his waistband and looked for another place to store it. Perhaps he would leave it behind in the car. He noticed the initials etched into the gun's butt. The sinking feeling in his stomach worsened.

"Stop de car. I gotta shit."

"Can't you hold it? Thirty minutes more to the truck stop."

"No. I'll just poop and make a mess in de car."

Groaning, Winston pulled off the highway and rolled into a Tim Horton's parking lot.

"We gotta give de money back," Ben said. His stomach stopped cramping the moment he said those words.

"What the fuck?"

"Yes."

"You crazy?"

"No. And we gotta take our punishment." The Benedictines were taking control. "Dis is wrong. De men in my family all fucked up. I hope our women will do better. I wish your mother was around."

Winston pounded the wheel, yelling at the top of his voice. "What the mother-fuck has gotten into you? Listen, old man—I am in charge here. I got more money riding on this deal than you have. Double!"

"Which you stole from your partner so you could brag to your old man?"

"You always said I could not make the big hit. Well, I done it!"

"Did I raise you all my life so you could show me how much better you are? Of course, I want you to be better. But not like dis. Where Elroy?"

"Elroy's a dumb fuck."

"He lent you his car. Is dat his dead body in de trunk stinking up de place?"

Winston paled and remained silent, staring at the fogging glass in front.

Ben pointed the gun in his hand—Elroy's gun—at his son. He hoped the gun would be persuasive where words were clearly failing him. He did not know even how to fire the damned thing. "We going back. I didn't bargain on murder. You killed your friend for de money. You stole his plan. Dat's not de way to play."

Winston swung his hand at Ben, a wild swing to deflect the old man's firearm, and the gun exploded inside the car.

In the close quarters, the sound was deafening. Winston and Ben were thrown back against their respective doors, only Winston ended up with a hole in his temple and the window on his side shattered with blood, brains following in its wake. Winston had finally caught his random bullet—from the most unlikely source.

"Oh fuck. Oh, holy shit," was all Ben could say as he jumped forward to embrace his son, to try to undo what had just transpired, putting fragments of bone and brain back where they should belong. "Why you did dat?"

People rushed out of the restaurant and peered into the car. Ben sighed and sat back cradling his dying son and cried, "Oh, Win, you going to a better place now. Oh, Win..."

His cries were soon drowned out by the wailing of sirens.

The lawyer closed his file. "I'm sorry to hear about all this. I hope the jury is sympathetic. Perhaps manslaughter might be more appropriate."

Ben shrugged. The talking had helped. "Dis only my words, anyway. Dey don't have to believe me. I not expecting anyone's mercy. But I have one favour to ask." He fished inside his pocket and pulled out a scrap of paper. "Find Cleo. Dis her mamma's last address in de Park."

The lawyer took the paper and looked closely at the writing. Then he put the paper in his pocket.

"Will Cleo still be able to use de RESP?" Ben asked.

"Sure. It's in her name, and it's portable. I wouldn't hold hope for your pension, though. Employers do not take kindly to employees who rob them. I'll see what I can do there, also."

Ben nodded. "Perhaps it's best dat Cleo start clean, after her education. No legacy. She should make it on her own. We men are fucked up. Now it's de turn of our women."

"Don't be hard on yourself. Your circumstances made you and Winston what you became. Cleo will have to face her own destiny, whatever that may be."

Ben bowed his head. "Thanks for listening."

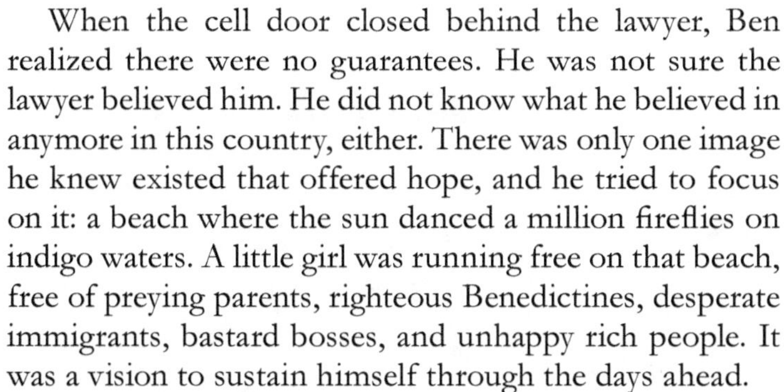

When the cell door closed behind the lawyer, Ben realized there were no guarantees. He was not sure the lawyer believed him. He did not know what he believed in anymore in this country, either. There was only one image he knew existed that offered hope, and he tried to focus on it: a beach where the sun danced a million fireflies on indigo waters. A little girl was running free on that beach, free of preying parents, righteous Benedictines, desperate immigrants, bastard bosses, and unhappy rich people. It was a vision to sustain himself through the days ahead.

SWINGERS

"We'll be discreet," Bob says as the plane circles turquoise waters and heads over coconut palms to land at the strip of airport. "Two weeks of sun, sand, and all-you-can-eat-and-drink on this Caribbean island. And sex? Hopefully."

Sandra is still not convinced this trip is a good idea, although at this stage she is willing to try anything to save their moribund, seven-year-old marriage that has produced no children, paid off their student loans, and landed them in mortgage debt. She glances at Bob who is sitting upright and eager, seatbelt tight against his growing paunch, only 35 and fully on the way to becoming a fat bald man, his crew-cut failing to hide the smoothness creeping beyond a wide forehead.

All work and no play for Bob: producing unbreakable computer code on a 24/7 schedule regulated by uppers and downers that have all but dried up his sexual desire, leaving her high and dry and pulling her hair out during her sexual peaks. Her dead mother would not have approved, but heck, she is 34 with no prospects of having a kid with "low-libido Bob", so why isn't she allowed to have sex on the brain at least?

She buckles her seatbelt and pulls it tight, hoping she does not put on weight during this vacation. She craves a cigarette; four hours on an aircraft is too long to have gone without one. To distract herself, she switches on her iPod and flicks to a selection of Calypso music—might as well get in the mood. Yet, her mind wanders to the events that led them to get on this plane...

It had started two weeks ago, after her mother's financial estate had been settled. Sandra returned home to their two-bedroom bungalow in the suburbs in the early afternoon and announced, "I've quit my admin assistant's job. You make so much money now, my contribution is irrelevant."

Bob raised an eyebrow from his computer. A nervous tic began above his right eye. "And what will you do?"

"I'm going to travel. I have never been to Europe."

He shut the laptop. "And leave me to manage the house?"

"It will be good for you. You can re-acquaint yourself with cooking, washing dishes, doing laundry, mowing the lawn, and shovelling snow."

"Hey, hey... this sounds like a *long* trip!"

"I'll travel until my inheritance runs out."

"Honey, this is ridiculous. This is not the rational way."

"You were never rational; you were always idealistic. And it seems to have paid off for you—giving up a safe bank IT job to become a well-paid hacker for a security firm. Now it's *my* turn."

He looked gloomily down at his coffee. "It's the sex, isn't it?"

"That… and other things. You don't hold me, anymore, Bob. We don't take walks. We don't talk. It's always work, work, and more work with you."

He rose and walked about the kitchen, looking at her occasionally. He opened his mouth a couple of times and closed it, looked at her again, and paced some more.

"You might as well say it," she said. "Your pacing is starting to make me nervous."

"You might think this is crazy, but I have been researching options for couples like us who are stuck in a rut."

"If the solution is watching porn movies—like I know you do on your laptop when you think I am not around—you can count me out!"

He blushed but came right back. "Well, I thought there was privacy around here. Not—I can see."

"I have no privacy, either, with your snoring and your ungodly work schedule."

"Hey, hey… let's not make this deteriorate into an argument. I'm good at what I do, that's why they hire me. Hackers never rest, nor do we. What I meant to say was… there are solutions for couples like us. For many couples like us. It's a form of honest group therapy."

She threw her head back and laughed. "Next you'll be suggesting 'swinging.'"

He held her gaze.

She stopped laughing.

"Why not?" he said.

"Are you crazy?"

"Honey, it is because I love you that I am proposing this. The carnal aspect of sex has gotten tame with us. We need to re-ignite it."

"And your porn doesn't do it for you anymore?"

"It's not the real thing. That's just a diversion from work."

Her curiosity was aroused. "And how do you propose we do this without getting a reputation as a couple of perverts?"

"Direct networking. There are tons of swinger networks rivalling the number of terrorist cells in this country. We plug into a network of a few like-minded couples our age, do candlelight dinners and such, and we are in. That's how it's done. Just like normal except dessert may have a different feel."

His seriousness fascinated her. She felt she still had to protest, so she rose and stormed out of the kitchen.

Two days later, she re-opened the discussion. "Where do we start?"

He looked up from his laptop; his "upper" medication was beginning to wear off, and he looked a bit foggy. "Start what?"

"Swinging."

"Oh!" His face came alight. "Now we are talking, are we?"

"I'm prepared to listen," she said and sat down on the chair across from his work desk, hands tight across her chest. He pulled up a travel website on his screen, zeroing down to an all-inclusive resort for couples in the Caribbean. "I'm told that many network members come here—recruiting, sampling even, before longer term commitments are made."

She leaned back in her chair and sighed. A curious elation hovered over her trepidation. "I guess we are going on holidays. When can you take time off?"

Crossing Limbo

The first day at the resort has gone by in a flurry of activity, beginning with lunch at the ocean-front buffet with an assortment of seafood, meats, pasta, rice, and desserts that made her tug at her black swimsuit to ensure there was still room. They were served a bottle of Chilean "vino blanco" which Bob hogged, along with several beers. She strolled the beach later while Bob floundered on a deckchair in the sun. The surf thundered under blue skies, and the warm winds were comforting and invigorating. Bodies of all kinds were on display, walking the endless beach that linked a string of tourist hotels; a few women—the shapely ones—had chosen to go topless.

As sunset falls, happy hour beckons, and generous quantities of cocktails are being doled out at the bar situated on an island in the middle of the swimming pool that meanders around the entire property. Sandra orders a *café con leche* from a surprised waiter while Bob easily picks up another beer from the ready supply on the man's tray. Bob's head nods dozily between sipping his beer.

"This is the life isn't it, honey?"

She doesn't want to remind him of why they came. In fact, she wonders if that other reason will simply go away. Perhaps, when Bob sobers up tomorrow, he may get romantic, especially since he has left his laptop at home. Although, he still has his Blackberry, and that worries her. Better yet, they may never meet members of the "Network", as she has started calling them, and this trip will end up as a good sun, sand, *sex*, and all-you-can-eat-and-drink holiday as she has been secretly hoping it would. There is still the spark of curiosity that had taken possession of her from the moment she had agreed to this trip and continues to plague her. Bob's mention of "swinging" has touched a nerve. Is she also just another carnal bitch like those topless women on the beach today who had flagrantly swung their tits at passing men?

But where are the members of the "Network" amidst this stream of elegantly dressed couples making their way out of their chalets and heading over to dinner at the various themed restaurants around the property? She begins to feel hungry.

"Bob, we'd better get showered and go to dinner." They are still in their swimwear. Even the diehard sun worshippers around the pool are collecting their belongings and staggering off to their rooms to change for the evening.

Sandra sees the smartly dressed couple heading their way.

The woman, in her early forties, is dressed in a black pantsuit with gold embroidery that sets off her lush black hair; a gold bracelet completes her finesse. The man, in his mid-forties, is thickset, muscular, and has close-cropped, curly, ash-grey hair; he is dressed in khaki pants and a white shirt with its top buttons undone to reveal a thick, black mop of chest hair. His tan shoes are designer-wear. As they pass, the woman inspects Bob, who is draining his beer and attempting to rise. The man looks Sandra over, his dark eyes boring into her, their intensity sending goose-bumps all over her. Never before has she brooked such appraisal. The woman shifts her gaze from Bob to Sandra and tilts her nose slightly. She bestows Sandra a disarming smile.

When the couple is out of earshot, Sandra grabs Bob, "Did you see them?"

Bob is still struggling to right himself, put on his sandals, and grab his beach bag and towel. "Who?"

She points. "Them. I think it's them—the 'Network.'"

"You're kidding." He stares. "How do you know?"

"I felt it."

"How did I look?"

"Still a bit drunk."

"Shit! I'd better shower then. I shouldn't have had so much sun on the first day."

She feels a pang of dismay. And yet... it is almost as if the adventure has begun—the hunt for some un-experienced pleasure.

The man's stare haunts her all the way through her shower. She feels him in the washroom with her, surveying her naked body, desiring her. Oh, it's been a long time since anyone desired her. Bob had... a long time ago. When she dries herself, she realizes that she is wet between her legs—not the kind of wetness that comes from the shower.

They hunt down the couple, peering into each of the restaurants and finding them in the Italian one named "Amore". Bob slips the maître d' a ten-dollar bill and manages to get a table within earshot. Sipping Chianti, they try to catch the older couple's conversation. The elegant man and the woman in black are wrapped in each other. Sandra catches snippets of conversation that come her way: references to Tuscany and then to Provence; they seem to have a villa or some abode in one or both locations.

"Do you think I wore the right clothes for this place?" Bob whispers in the dim candlelight of their table, leaning forward lest he be overheard. He is wearing a golf shirt and jeans. The smartly dressed hostess had looked at Bob in dismay, yet invited them in—after all they were paid guests, and tourism was important to this island.

"You could spiff it up a notch the next time," Sandra says. She is wearing a V-necked red top that reveals her cleavage and a necklace of seashells she bought at the gift shop soon after arrival.

"You are right. It is them," Bob says.

"They don't look very interested, other than in each other. It's not how they looked at us the first time."

"Like you said, I can *feel* it. The book says this is how it works: initial interest, then disinterest, then interest—the dance." Bob looks like a lapdog waiting for the slightest scrap of attention from its master.

"She's too old for you," Sandra says.

"She is sexy. It oozes from her disinterested pores."

"You don't feel that way with me? You did once."

"Honey, slow down. We have been through this before. We have come here for a lift in our sex lives. How's the guy?"

"He's okay." She tries to feign indifference, but the man at the other table is making her sweat.

The other couple push away their espresso cups. The woman nods, and the man turns and heads over to their table. Sandra quickly averts her eyes, for she has been caught staring. They've both been staring, right through dinner.

The man bows in front of their table. Both Sandra and Bob struggle to rise. "No, please be seated. My name is Nikos Kosta. My wife, Sylvana, and I would like your company for breakfast tomorrow at nine a.m." He gestures with his hand towards his wife.

From across the way, the woman in black gives Bob and Sandra a wide smile.

Before he leaves their table, Nikos adds, "We are going to the adult show at the theatre. Tonight's performance is highly recommended."

Sandra and Bob fidget over breakfast at the sea-grill restaurant the following morning. Their newfound friends are late. Or have they arrived too early? Sandra checks her watch—9:15 a.m.

Sandra had been too keyed-up to sleep last night. So much was happening in a very short time. Bob had pounced on her the moment they arrived back at their chalet after the show. He made love vigorously and earthily, but had climaxed too soon. Then, this morning, he was at it again, lasting a little longer but nowhere close to the one hour clocked, oh, so long ago. If this is what swinging was supposed to do, it was working, even in small doses. Or was it prompted by the all-nude dance review they had seen at the theatre last night—Nikos' recommendation—Caribbean mulatto men and women with only coloured plumes covering their private parts, prancing around to throbbing salsa music? As the music reached its crescendo, the costumes were shed, and the stage transformed into a mass of writhing glistening bodies whose energies radiated and engulfed the audience in a musky headiness. Open-mouthed in amazement, Bob had rubbed Sandra's leg throughout the performance. Nikos and Sylvana were seen fleetingly in the front row, but they were studying the performance rather clinically.

When the other couple arrive at 9:20, Sylvana is wearing a red beach wrap, sandals, and dark glasses pushed back on her head; her hair is held together with a red scarf. Her nipples, full and large, poke through the thin fabric. Nikos is dressed in a tight white singlet and blue beach shorts; his thick legs are as hairy as his chest.

"So sorry for the delay," Nikos says, pulling a chair out for Sylvana. "I had an unexpected call from the office even though I asked them not to call me. Please accept my apologies."

"No problem," Bob stumbles, all smiles, stealing sly glimpses at Sylvana who is playing with her wrap, tightening it behind her neck. Sandra feels self-conscious at this well depilated woman and wonders if she has stubble under her own arms that she shaved only yesterday before heading to the airport.

"Did you enjoy the show last night?" Sylvana looks at Bob and Sandra. Her voice is like a purring cat.

"It was... bold," Sandra says.

Breakfast lasts an hour. Sylvana eats only cereal and fruit while Nikos has liberal helpings of eggs, ham, and orange juice. Bob tries to emulate Nikos. Sandra sticks to toast and marmalade—she has lost the appetite she had yesterday, before she met this couple.

They are consultants; Nikos runs a management consulting company, and Sylvana is a home designer. They have a condo in Toronto and a villa in Tuscany and are considering buying a studio in France but are deciding between Giverny and Provence. They have no children, and they travel a lot.

Over the last dregs of coffee, Sandra pops the pressing question, ignoring Bob's kick under the table. "Why did you select us last night?"

"You looked like you were seeking," Sylvana says. "We recognize that in people. We were seeking too, once."

"And did you find?" Bob asks, his eyes bulging.

"Oh, yes. That truism 'seek and you will find' works. See that man and woman over there?" Sylvana motions over to an older man and a young woman sitting at a table in the far corner. "Her husband is over on the other side with her present companion's wife. They arrived and met three days ago."

"I could never have told, "Sandra exhales.

"So, what happens now? I mean, between us?" Bob bursts out.

Sandra wants to kick him under the table, but a perverse curiosity holds her back.

"Nothing. You go about your activities here in the resort and let your curiosity and excitement mount. Until this evening. We will meet you for dinner, and we can go to the show together. There is also dancing at the pool afterwards, which I recommend." Sylvana twirls a prune in her mouth and bites down on it; the black juice spills out of the sides of her mouth, and she smiles at Bob before wiping it off with her napkin.

On the other side of the table, Nikos, who has been nursing a look of quiet amusement, turns his appraisal on Sandra, and she feels that same scrutiny from yesterday, his eyes penetrating through her thin cheesecloth shirt, cutting through the straps of her bikini underneath, shedding it.

She catches his gaze and stares back into his dark eyes. She feels herself melting under his smile, wanting him, despite Bob sitting next to her. She takes a sip of water to get back to reality. *This is crazy!* She has never been this way before.

"Now you must excuse us." Sylvana tosses her napkin on the table and rises. "It's time for my massage. And Nikos is going for his golf game. It was really nice meeting you. Do give this some thought, and if you wish to continue, meet us for dinner. We are dining at the French restaurant this evening at seven."

When they leave, Sandra throws her napkin on the table. "This is just over the top for me."

"Hey, hey. Come on. We knew this was a strange country."

"But Bob—if... if those two couples over there end up separating, or going off with other people, this whole exercise would have been in vain."

"Well, Sylvana and Nikos haven't. They have been married fifteen years—they said so. See how solid and confident they are together."

Sandra gets up from the table and heads for their room. She wants to get away from this inevitable situation they are rushing headlong into, alternately restrained by conscience yet spurred on by a carnal curiosity born of the sexual malaise of their last couple of years.

For the rest of the day, she indulges in all the diversions a vacation resort can provide: she catamarans; she rides astride the banana boat that takes a group of tourists out to sea and tips them overboard, the tow boat captain laughing over the side as his charges wallow in the water, safe in their life vests but surprised nevertheless at being in the wide ocean, prey to marauding sharks and other predators. "Don't worry—there are no sharks. The sharks are only in the mind," laughs the captain over the side. They claw their way up quickly to regain seating positions on the banana boat and are towed back to shore. Later,

Sandra goes parasailing, and as her parachute sails over the beach, littered with a myriad of semi-nude bodies, she wonders how much sex these people will be having with each other in the privacy of their rooms—or other people's rooms—later in the day. The ordered civility of this beach is a smokescreen. Can anyone be trusted for what they appear to be? She looks over the sea of bodies to see if she can catch sight of Bob. He had been too scared to take the parasail or ride the banana boat and had contented himself to laze on the beach with an instant-refill beer mug.

She skips lunch and walks down to the small town just outside the resort. A lorry passes by in a haze of dust and screeches to a halt by a fenced construction site. A crush of native workers in hardhats rush to board the bus. Some fall off in the melee. The bus fills up quickly, with everyone standing and grabbing any rail for stability. The driver screams at those left behind to stop clinging to the bus. The vehicle takes off in another blast of dust, with bodies clutching, jolting, some even giving up and letting go. The ones left behind curse and swear and head back to the site to wait for the next transport.

Native women, with babies strapped around their backs, sell wooden trinkets along the narrow main street of the town; each one seems to have the same wares: watercolour paintings, wooden carvings, cloth scarves, maracas, seashell bangles, and necklaces. The babies are crying or have fallen into an apathetic sleep. Some of the women pursue Sandra aggressively, asking her to buy, and she hurries her step. At an open bar, native men drink rum, smoking foul-smelling cigars and look dazed; the yet-sober ones wolf-whistle at her. She ducks into a curio shop and buys a set of hand-painted, wooden bangles and some postcards. The cashier cannot make change for her dollars so Sandra tells her to keep the change. Perhaps that has been deliberate on the cashier's part, Sandra does not know, but she feels she has made a charitable contribution to this Third World economy. She senses the overbearing poverty of this place and shrugs at the irony that just on the other side of the wall is the cocooned resort where food of every kind is available in unlimited supply, and its denizens are left to indulge in passions that are far from normal. She passes a motel beside the open-air market, a hole in the wall with a brightly hand-painted sign advertising that "breakfast is included". As she passes, a tourist couple emerges from its confines. The young man and woman have Canadian flags on their backpacks and look like university students.

"How's it going?" Sandra asks.

The guy—pimply faced and unshaven—smiles. "Great. The hiking in the hills is fantastic." He reminds her of the boys she dated in university before meeting Bob: safe, immature, predictable.

The girl, wearing a yellow bandana across her head, is plump and wears glasses. "The volcano has some of the best trails."

"Is that where you are headed?" Sandra asks.

"Yeah. We will be camping overnight and then climbing up to the crater early tomorrow morning."

"Is it safe?"

"Safer than down here," the girl says.

"Is your accommodation okay?"

"Oh, I didn't mean that the accommodation is unsafe— it's run by a local family. Very nice and as comfortable as they can make it. It's out on the street that's unsafe."

"The people here look deprived," the boy says. "Our landlady says she is unable to buy food sometimes as everything is reserved for the resorts."

"But breakfast is included—the sign says so," Sandra points out.

"Oh yes—fruit mainly—that's the only thing that's plentifully available. And fish. We are a bit fed up with salt fish for breakfast." The girl giggles.

Sandra bids them a good hike, lights a cigarette, and resumes her walk. The cigarettes give her no satisfaction; they just have to be lit when the craving button goes off in her head.

She joins Bob down on the beach around four o'clock. He is unhealthily red in places, sizzled. He is on his cell phone. He rises and walks some distance from her, talking intently into the phone. She resents him bringing the phone, but his "business" cannot let him be without it. He looks crestfallen when he puts down the device.

"Bad news from 'Hackers Inc'?" she teases.

"Oh, shut up. They are legit. I told you that."

"Well, you look like shit."

"I haven't been sleeping well. The heat. And I think I took too much sun today again."

She cannot resist another jibe. "Sylvana may pass you over tonight."

He feels the stubble on his jaw. "Gotta take a shave. For once, the guys back home can figure things out." He hurries off to sober up. When she eventually goes into their bedroom, he is snoring on the bed, his hair wet from the shower.

She wonders if he is still on those uppers and downers, yet is reluctant to look inside his giant toiletry case. She is losing her grip on understanding Bob. Even understanding herself. She sits by the bed and stares at him.

Will this work? Or is she putting her bet on a loser? This whole island is unreal compared to the ordered egalitarian world she knows back home.

"Why do you swing?" Sandra asks Sylvana boldly. They are at the poolside bar. Dinner and the show are over, and their men are getting drinks as they sit at a table away from the floodlights bathing the pool area. Couples sway languorously to salsa beats from a hyperactive DJ.

Throughout dinner, Nikos had made small talk with her, complimenting Sandra on the new bangles she had bought, showing an interest in her recounting of her walk into the town, of her adventures in the banana boat, and of the exhilaration of the parasail. She had drunk a couple of glasses of wine during dinner and is feeling less nervous, more adventurous. Nikos is looking less threatening. He actually seemed like an okay guy as the evening progressed. He suggested that Bob give his firm a call to discuss a software consulting gig. Bob beamed with pride, and the worried look he had nursed since receiving the call from Toronto evaporated. When they sat down at the pool, Sandra lit a cigarette while the men left to get more drinks Now, she thinks it is time to get to the point.

"Why do we swing?" Sylvana chews on the question, dangling the umbrella toothpick, from her empty margarita glass, in her mouth. She is casually, but stylishly, dressed: red and green flowered skirt, plain white, sleeveless, cotton top, and matching white scarf, pearl necklace and bangles, and red sandals. "It has kept us together. Contrary to public opinion, men are not the only polygamous humans. Besides it doesn't hurt anyone. It's consensual."

"Isn't it addictive?"

"Isn't anything that is pleasurable addictive—chocolate, alcohol, tobacco, fatty food, tea?"

"Do you and Nikos enjoy sex together?"

Sylvana leaves the question unanswered while Nikos and Bob walk towards them juggling drinks in their hands. Before the men arrive, Sylvana leans over the table towards Sandra. "Listen, if you are not a hundred percent certain, don't do it. Nikos likes you, and I know you will enjoy having sex with him. If you are not sure, just get up from this table and walk away. We will no doubt be disappointed and have to start again. I will understand."

The men are at their table, and Sandra gulps half of her brandy, hoping it will drive away any doubts and make her decision easier.

"Dance with me, Bobby," Sylvana raises her hand towards Bob.

"My pleasure." Bob downs his scotch and hauls Sylvana onto the dance floor where the tempo has changed to a rumba.

Sandra feels a warm hand, like a paw, engulf hers. Nikos's face is looming, and his hot breath, tinged with garlic and anisette, overpowers her. "You look very beautiful tonight, Cassandra."

During her youth, she may have shrugged that off as a corny pick-up line. But Cassandra? The lover of Apollo? And under this gentle tropical moon with the surf beating in the background, still audible above the sensuous rumba rhythms? She throws back the rest of her brandy and feels carefree. She is not going to leave this table and head for her room—she is too far gone. When Nikos proposes they dance, she stubs her cigarette, takes his hand, and steps out aggressively onto the dance floor.

He spins her gently towards him and away, swaying his hips—for a big man he is nimble. She stares at his half-unbuttoned shirt, at the tangle of hair bursting forth, and breathes in his manly smell when he brings her in close, pressing her to his body. Already his crotch is hard when she makes fleeting contact, and his face has a half-smile, almost a leer.

He presses his lips to her ear, and his tongue, heavy and wet, is licking her inner lobe. Her nipples stand out, and she is getting furiously wet in all orifices. Yet he draws out this dance, slowly swinging her out and bringing her in, until she wants to scream, "Take me. Take me!"

At the end of the second piece, he steers her away from the dance floor, and she starts to cool down. "To my room," he commands, and she obeys, glad the foreplay is over.

The brandy is making her head spin, and the walk is a confluence of ground lights, stars, and chalet lights. She is indoors now, a door clicks shut behind her, the lock turns, the exterior lights are replaced by dimmer interior ones. Her clothes peel off her body and hands run over her tingling flesh; a mouth, hot and wet, engulfs her nipples, swelling them to bursting point, travels down her stomach to her clit, parting hair, mixing moisture—his with hers—stroking, igniting. She grabs his head of thick, oily, curly hair and smashes him into her cunt. "Fuck me!" she shrieks involuntarily, and she falls back on cool sheets, panting as he enters her vigorously and deliberately. She comes in a flood, yet his hard shaft persists, rubbing, thrusting rhythmically, and his hot breath releases an unpleasant odour—frightening, overpowering.

She wants him to stop. She is satiated, but he holds her down with powerful hands and grinds her harder and harder until her insides feel they are going to tear apart. "Let me go" she wails. "Please, take a break."

"No, my lady—this is what making love is all about," he says in a measured tone and continues his torment.

For her, the pleasure has evaporated.

She loses track of time, momentarily. When she shakes herself awake, she has been spun around and that giant cock is pressing against her ass. "No," she screams but is powerless as his strength forces her down.

Pain shoots through her, and she does not know, yet, if this is also a part of intense pleasure.

She has no control. Just as she is about to let go and pass out with the pain, Nikos retracts, leaving her deflated. She rolls over to the side of the bed, and he staggers off somewhere else in the room with a continuous stream of diminishing "ahhs" bouncing off the walls. She wants to sleep, to block out what has taken place, but her body starts to tingle again as the pain eases. Sitting bolt upright in bed, all vestiges of pleasure, horniness, and pain fall off her—replaced by a sense of deep dread.

Nikos emerges from the washroom, a towel strung across his neck, naked; his thick cock dangling contentedly against his right thigh. "Did you enjoy it?" He grins. His casualness after what he has just done to her makes him resemble Judas, her Judas.

Moving gingerly, she gathers her clothes from the various corners of the room, feeling raw and torn. She needs to get out of this place; the bitterness in her mouth increases the sense of suffocation in the room.

"It is always like that—the first time without your regular partner," his voice is dawdling, coaxing. "But you get used to it. In fact, you seek it more and more."

She has bra and panties on and wriggles into her skirt, strings her top over her shoulders and stumbles to the door.

"Please do not go back to your room. Sylvana and Bob will be there."

His words hit her like a hammer. She remembers her shoes and reaches with her hands for where she thinks they dropped off her feet but can't find them. Her hands clutch a man's shoe instead. She flings it with all her might at Nikos. "You bastard! You filthy bastard!"

As she stumbles out of the chalet, she hears his voice cooing after her, "So temperamental... perhaps we talk again tomorrow, eh? You will feel better in the morning. Breakfast at eight?'

She staggers towards her room then checks herself. Bob and Sylvana. Her lip curls in disgust. She turns and heads towards the beach bar. The cool sand under her bare feet is soothing. She drives her toes deep into it for comfort and lets the grains cascade off her feet. The wind off the ocean is gusty, and she shivers and pulls on her cotton top, a couple of the buttons have come off—the bastard must have ripped them. Or did she, at the height of her heat? She feels deep shame for her carnality. Why? It is human nature. But... it did not have to manifest like this. She craves a cigarette but has none on her.

The bartender is wrapping up for the night, the last of the patrons having gone seeking other pleasures.

"One more for the night, Miss?" He looks knowingly at her. He has seen people like her before, she realizes, trysts that have not gone off so well.

"Double brandy."

"Coming up." He places the glass in front of her and is generous in his serving—the glass is full. "Don't go swimming in the ocean after this, Miss. I've seen many people do. It's not worth it." He continues cleaning up, shutting off the bar lights.

She rinses her mouth with the brandy, letting the spirits scour every cranny, and spits it out into the sand. She feels a bit cleaner. The barman raises his eyes and shrugs as she strips her clothes off. She does not feel embarrassment for her nudity in front of this stranger; she has gone too far for that now. She walks into the ocean. The water is warm and soothing, like the sand has been, washing away the fluids on and inside her body, cleaning her with its salty indifference. She floats on her back, looking upward at an upside down three-quarter moon, trying to reconcile its tranquility with what goes on below in this island paradise. She figures out that she will never know. She is one of those humans too, and there is no escape. Or is there?

Cassandra, the lover of Apollo. The other part of that mythological story, learned long ago in school, returns— Apollo cursed Cassandra when she spurned him, reducing her to a life of pain and frustration.

She wades out of the water, returns to the bar, and retrieves her drink and clothes.

"You won't be doing anything stupid, would you, Miss?" The bartender has his hands on his hips, a rope and life vest are slung over his shoulder. He must have been observing her while she skinny-dipped.

"I'll be all right now," she says.

"If you are going to sit by the water, watch the tide come in—take your deck chair up the beach." He tosses the vest and rope behind the bar counter and switches off the remaining bar light. "I'll bid you a goodnight, Miss. Remember—it is not worth it!"

When she next looks back, he is gone.

She finishes her brandy in long sips, sitting in a chair dragged up the beach to where the water only makes eddies underneath her. The water keeps her awake and sober, and her life with Bob flashes before her with every rush in of the tide. Bob has been a tide, nothing good from him stays, the gifts of his experiences with her are like those patterns left behind in the sand, impermanent, easily swept away by the beach cleaners the next morning.

Sometime near dawn she must have dozed for the next time she is conscious, a gentle hand is shaking her.

"Sandra, my dear. Are you okay?"

Sandra opens her eyes. Sylvana is stooping over her. She has showered and is wearing a blue beach wrap under which a black bikini peeps out; blue sandals and a matching scarf complete her accoutrements. The sun is a pink glow emerging from the horizon in the east.

"What time is it?" Sandra stretches her cramped body.

"It's coming on six o'clock. People will be walking the beach soon. I came when I couldn't find you in our room."

"How's Bob," Sandra feels her lip curl involuntarily when she thinks of Bob and Sylvana coupling.

"Sleeping soundly. He enjoyed me although he has much to learn. I think he has potential in this game."

Sandra is aghast at the detachment in Sylvana's voice.

"He seems like an object to you. Is that what this is?"

"My dear—this is all about selfish pleasure. Either you have this capability, or you don't. Bob is a very self-centred young man—he will do well in this circuit. You second guess yourself. You should have walked away last night."

Sandra looks out into the ocean. A few walkers are starting to emerge from their rooms, heading for the water.

Sylvana straightens up. "Well, it is time for my yoga on the beach. I suggest you get some real shut-eye. You look pretty worn out. Nikos has that effect on inexperienced women."

"Inexperienced! I have been married for seven years."

"Yes—but you are still inexperienced. You asked me if Nikos and I have a good sex life, and I never got a chance to reply last night. Well—if it's any consolation to you— we don't sleep with each other anymore. Our gratification is in the new, not the tried and true. Bram Stoker once wrote a book about it. Stoker made one mistake however, we don't suck new blood—we seek it! Despite Bob's fumbling last night, I got more satisfaction from him than I can get from Nikos. Does that answer you?"

Sylvana turns on her heel and takes measured paces down the beach, walking into the rising sun.

Sandra rises and walks back to her room. She is hungry, but the all-you-can eat buffet does not interest her anymore. The smell of cooking: eggs, ham, bacon, and barbecued meat coming out of the open-air grill sickens her. She hurries along.

Bob is snoring when she enters, contented and innocent in his slumber. She recognizes that look; in the early days of their marriage, when he had satiated himself on good sex, he used to look like that. He stirs, opens an eye, sees her, and rolls over. He is snoring again in no time. What happened to the renewed desire in their relationship that last night was supposed to evoke? All she feels for him right now is a deep revulsion.

She goes to the closet, takes out her suitcase, and begins to pack her things. She tries not to wake him. She feels no remorse or regret; seeing him sprawled and cocooned in his satisfied body makes it easier to leave. She hopes the bed and breakfast place has a vacancy.

The cell phone rings sharply, shaking them both. Bob rolls his eyes, trying to get his bearings, then grabs the phone. He shouts, "Shit! Shutting us down?"

She tiptoes to the door while he yells into the phone. "Fuck you!" He throws the cell phone across the room— it hits the sofa and bounces into a corner. Gone is the look of innocent contentment on his face, replaced with a scowl. He notices her for the first time, by the door, suitcase in hand. No explanation is necessary; his scowl turns into a howl.

"No, Sandy baby, not you, too! This was all wrong, wasn't it? Let's go back. Let's start again."

"It's too late for that now, Bob. Sylvana and Nikos opened up new doors in us I didn't think we had. She thinks you have a future in swinging. And Nikos can get you a new IT job. Good-bye!"

She slams the door behind her and walks down the paved pathway towards the large gates that lead out of the property. Maybe she'll head out to the volcano to get away from all this, until her charter flight back to Toronto. She holds back the tears and the desire to turn back—they must be controlled, like the urge to smoke, and that *other* feeling in the pit of her stomach. She just wishes she can hold all these forces at bay while she works through this split. Above all, she must not cave in. She knows Bob will not come after her, even though he will rant and rave for a while—he has seen how determined she is. Besides, he has Sylvana and other swingers to distract him. He must be re-calibrating his options, planning his next move—people like Bob did not stay down for too long. Like Sylvana had said, Bob is a thoroughly self-centred individual.

A blond young man steps out of his chalet along the path she is walking down. He is dressed in a bikini brief, suntan lotion glistening on his sculpted body, his crotch bursting for release from its skimpy confines. He stretches in the morning rays and looks at her. He smiles. She feels the rush of desire in her body, stronger than she has ever felt before. She resists the urge to pounce, tear that fragile piece of G-string from his body and devour him. *The sharks are in the mind.* Instead, she asks, "Got a cigarette?"

He looks surprised, even repelled. "I don't smoke," he says.

"Of course." *With that beautiful body, you should not.*

She shivers and passes him, her shoulders hunched. The gate to the outside world seems very far away.

Shane Joseph

POSTCARDS FROM WATER'S EDGE

I found the postcards towards the end of my visit to the cottage.

I'd been on the downer since that bastard Higgins called me into his office and told me my career was over. Twenty years I'd given to that ungrateful company; twenty years of maintaining their computers, getting up at all times of the night whenever troubleshooting was required. I'd been a 24/7 help-desk all by myself, sometimes more for my own security than the firm's. And then he'd had the audacity to...

"We're outsourcing to India," Higgins had said, looking out of the window of his cavernous office. "It's not about you, Jim."

"Can I go work for Mark over in Product Development?" I pleaded. Mark and his team were forever making new products, but they had no technical aptitude whatsoever.

"I'm afraid that won't be possible. Mark's team is being outsourced, too. Design is going to China and development to India. Welcome to globalization."

This was, after all, 2008, the year capitalism in the west went into decline, never to return to its former glory.

When I got home that day, my marriage also ended. My artsy wife, Nancy, who painted, hobnobbed with gallery owners in Toronto, sold nothing, and lived off my steady income was shocked at my unemployed status.

"How will we live?"

"You mean, how will *you* live?" I growled. In retrospect, I should not have said that. But I had not been fired before, so I had no examples to draw from.

A fierce row ensued, followed by a lengthy silence, and my relegation to the spare bedroom which I had become very familiar with in recent years. Nancy left the following week to live with a "friend." I found out soon after that this friend owned a gallery and had been "thinking" of doing a show exclusively for Nancy. After her move-in—or move-out from me—the show was confirmed. At least I did not have to worry about Nancy anymore.

Alice, a co-worker in my IT area, called to enquire how I was doing, just as I was pouring my fourth scotch the day Nancy left. Alice had always been solicitous about me in the ten years we had worked together. She had volunteered frequently to take the graveyard helpdesk shifts from me as she had no significant-other in her life and was half-a-dozen years younger than me. I think she heard the plaintive tone in my voice over the phone—I had never had four scotches in a day, either—and suggested I take a break and put some space between me and my troubles.

"My family has a cottage out in Haliburton. It's a bit rundown but should give you a change of scene," she said. "You could have it for a week."

"In summer? Isn't there high demand for cottages? In whatever shape they are in? I don't want to put anyone out."

"We don't know what to do with the place at the moment. It was my grandmother's. After she died in the 80s, the place has never been the same. My generation is not that dedicated to upkeep. We are thinking of selling it. So, if you can take a bit of rusticity, it's yours for a week next month—free of charge."

That's how I arrived at *Water's Edge*, this cottage on the lake, and met the ghost of Margaret.

As Alice had said, *Water's Edge* was rustic but not run-down. Its main structure was a wooden A-frame with fittings that had enjoyed their height of grandeur in the 60s. The most ornate pieces were in the dining room on the land side of the main building: solid oak table, cane-backed chairs, and intricate lampshades coated in a fine film of dust. The living room of the A-frame extended almost to the water's edge—hence the name of the cottage, I guessed—looking out onto the large lake with its far bank almost out of sight and shrouded in mist. The cottage smelled of aging wood, uncared for, yet generous and warm. I felt immediately at home.

A more recent extension on the side provided a kitchen, TV room, master bedroom, and bathroom. The five-acre property was overgrown and sprawling and had many buildings scattered about it: a studio, a boathouse, a garage, and other assorted sheds that were shut and cluttered with old furniture, equipment, and personal effects. Tall grass crept everywhere, threatening the long, tree-shrouded gravel driveway leading off the main road.

After I unpacked my things, which included a liberal supply of alcohol, I sat down in the living room and sipped my first scotch of the evening, watching the boaters and sea-doers retire to their respective cottages along the lake, reducing mechanized noise on the water and ushering in the natural sounds of slapping waves and the occasional loon. A full moon rising over the treeline cast a golden beam of shimmering light across the water. That beam seemed to target me and, wherever I moved inside the cottage, it followed me through the open windows—perhaps the gods were trying to send me a message, or the Devil was trying to strike me down. After my third scotch, I did not bother too much about old Lucifer.

The phone rang. I had some difficulty locating it. It was on the kitchen table, buried under the groceries I had brought with me and still had not stored away.

It was Alice. "Jim, how's everything? Hope you found the light switches and hope the hot water is working. I asked the neighbour to fire everything up, including propane in the barbecue outside."

"Everything's fine," I declared.

I guess I was already slurring my words, for she said, "Don't take it too hard. Others have had tougher roads."

"Are you still employed with the firm?"

"They are keeping me, they said. They need someone to train the Indians. They even—"

"They'll have to sell their bloody products to the Indians, too. People in Canada will all be on welfare and shopping at the thrift store before long."

"You can write your novel now." She giggled.

"Have not had much of a life to write one. And now the best parts are shot."

"Then you can write Grandma's. I wish she had written it. There was so much I wanted to learn from her. I was a rebellious teenager when she died. I was more interested in parties and getting drunk in those days."

"And I seem to be just rediscovering my teenage years," I said, pouring my fourth shot. "I was too studious. Planned the big career, four kids, a big house in the burbs, a Cadillac, and a boat. Oh, and a wife to help make all that happen. Ended up with a Chevy Cobalt and a mortgaged condo. No kids because Nancy was too busy painting. No Caddy—couldn't afford it. And certainly no boat—way out of my league. And now, no bloody career, either. And no wife! I wish I could start again."

"But you can. You must."

I knew she was only trying to be conciliatory. "Don't kid me, Alice. I am fifty-one. That's over the hill in corporate-speak."

"Grandma Margaret lived to be one-hundred-and-two, and she had many lives and many careers—nurse, gardener, housewife, mother, church warden, shop owner, hotelier to name a few. She worked into her late eighties. When she retired to the cottage, she wanted to convert it into a resort in time for her hundredth birthday, but we put it down to her creeping Alzheimer's."

"That was another generation. We are yuppies, Alice— we wanted it all and ended up with nothing."

"You know, Jim—you are beginning to depress me. I have to go. I will look in on you from time-to-time. Go slow, get lots of sun, and relax. Bye."

I was sad to hear her hang up. She was the closest thing I had to a friend, someone who stood by you when the chips were down. I wondered where the guys in the golf club were, or the bridge team? None had called since I was canned; probably out recruiting a new member to join their fraternity so they could continue indulging in the old jock jokes.

I promised myself I would not drive Alice away with anymore depressing talk. She was my lifeline, and I was not going to sever that.

It rained the next day—a great thunderstorm, knocking out the satellite TV. I was already tired of the detective novel I had picked up at Walmart, and so I decided to wander the cottage, checking out my surroundings, trying to get a feel for the denizens who had passed through this place.

The bookshelves that were amply spread out across the house had a jumble of books and magazines, mainly on gardening, DYI home maintenance, cooking, knitting, and one on birth control written in the 1920s. Three books caught my attention: *How to Write your Life Story*, *Writing for Fun*, and *Everyone can be a Writer.* There were underlined pages and annotations in neat cursory writing in the margins. There was no handwritten memoir lurking about, however, or any attempted writing by an amateur to be seen.

When the rain eased, I went into the studio. The smell of turpentine was strong. Scaling over a mountain of snow removal equipment, old paint cans, and garden tools, I arrived at another bookshelf that lined a whole wall. A collected *Life* series of all the countries of the world ran two rows. Another couple of rows were dedicated to a *Life* series on topics from Agriculture to Zoology. More books on gardening, healthcare, entrepreneurship, tennis, golf, hospitality—all with copious notes in the margins in the same feminine, cursive script, made with different ink, perhaps at different times. A series of register books lined the lower rows. Skimming through them, I saw the same handwriting: unknown names and addresses and room numbers that did not go beyond the number ten. There was always a Mr. and Mrs. of the same surname or a single name per room. Each register covered a year for the period 1946 to 1956.

Stepping out of the studio into the moist air, I had the guilty feeling I was spying on someone's life. It had been a full life, with many starts and stops, many pathways, many beginnings. It was as if every time she began—by now I was sure this was Grandma Margaret—she had to learn things from scratch. I resolved to snoop a bit every day, for diversion, and with a bit of envy.

That night, when I retired to bed I studied the photographs that circled the walls of the master bedroom. I had been so drunk on the night of my arrival that I had just fallen across the soft bed and snored until morning. Family portraits stretching back several generations. Margaret's parents were English and Scottish immigrants who had come to Canada in the second half of the 19th century. Stern-looking people, hardy, and florid. Margaret was born in 1884, the youngest of eight children, protected and ensconced within a strong family. Later portraits show a teenaged Margaret in a flowing dark gown and a blown black mass of hair, standing next to a dwindled number of siblings; perhaps some had grown up and gone away or died. In the early portraits, Margaret's dark eyes radiate a luminescence, a capacity for deep feeling; her jaw is firm and outthrust with confidence and daring. A handsome woman, a strong one.

Continuing down the years, there were pictures of a maturing Margaret with a smiling man by her side. Each picture had a different man, and each picture had a different setting: the oldest one being outside a church with

Margaret in a bridal gown; the next on a tennis court with Margaret in matching white short skirt, collared sleeveless vest, socks, and tennis shoes; the third on a golf course; and the last one on a cruise ship. Her surname under each of the photographs was different, uncharacteristic of the earlier impression I had formed of her. The most recent picture in the room, dated 1985, the year before she died, showed a frail and shrunken Margaret in the centre, still daring the world with her outthrust jaw, surrounded by many generations of family whose connections I could not get, except that I saw a younger, slimmer Alice in jeans and a spaghetti-strapped top—she had breasts I could make out; at the office she always hid them under business jackets and sweaters—with an Afro hairstyle, hovering on the fringe of the gathering.

I phoned Alice the next morning.

"How are you?" she said a bit breathless, even before I said hello. I guess she had Call Display or had been waiting expectantly for me to call.

"Oh, fine. I was calling to enquire about your grandmother."

"Oh." She sounded disappointed, only mildly enthusiastic.

"She had many last names. Adams, Pope, Johnson, Anderson, and Smith."

"She had four husbands. Adams was her maiden name."

"I see. So, she went through divorce, too?"

"No. They all died, as far as I know. The husbands, I mean. Johnson, the second husband, was my mother's father. Anderson, the third husband, only lasted five years, or so Mum said, before he died of an aneurism. He had started the hotel that Grandma continued to run after his death. I only remember the last one, Grandpa Smith. He was married to Margaret the longest and loved to sail. He was a retired insurance broker, always had a lot of money. He died of lung cancer when I was ten. He was a jolly man, used to write poetry and smoked a pipe. Grandma retired to the cottage after he died, puttered away in her garden, and did volunteer work."

"What about Pope, the first husband?"

"I don't know. Grandma did not speak much about him except to say he had been a photographer, and she had been widowed when she married my grandfather, Bob Johnson, who was a school principal at the time and a tennis coach. But Grandpa Johnson died before I was born. Why are you so interested?"

I did not know the answer. Perhaps when you lose something you go in search of something else to cling onto—just like Margaret had done. In this deserted cottage, the ghost of this ancient woman was the only thing I could tangibly hold onto, and I was pursuing her. I could not tell this to Alice, of course.

"I could come over this weekend, if you like. There is something I want to tell you. And we could go through some of her old postcards," Alice offered.

"Postcards?"

"Yes. They tell a great story. Grandma was threatening to turn them into a memoir, but she was always busy with something else. It was as if she were trying to find an excuse not to write it. Her dramatic death alone would be a fitting close for any book."

"How did she die?"

"She was found in her nightdress, floating in her canoe on the lake one winter's morning. Her caregiver, who slept in the studio, hadn't heard a sound. We figured that Grandma had woken in the middle of the night, in a demented state, and thought that she could go out for a paddle in her boat. Only, it was just above freezing at the time."

"The stuff of a novel."

"That's why I think it needs to be written. Maybe one day I'll get to it."

"I'll buy some wine for when you come out," I said, realizing that Margaret had been dominating our conversation thus far.

"That would be nice." Alice's voice became coy. "White, please."

"Sure."

When I put down the phone, I felt unbelievably light. It was as if I had been engaged with two angels, a live one and her dead grandmother.

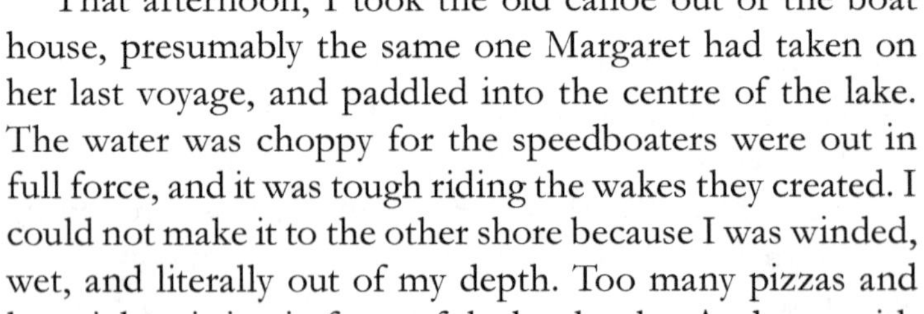

That afternoon, I took the old canoe out of the boat house, presumably the same one Margaret had taken on her last voyage, and paddled into the centre of the lake. The water was choppy for the speedboaters were out in full force, and it was tough riding the wakes they created. I could not make it to the other shore because I was winded, wet, and literally out of my depth. Too many pizzas and late nights sitting in front of the boob tube. And now with all the booze... I did not take a drink that evening.

The next morning, I found a bicycle in the garage, rusty and creaky. A bit of engine oil lying nearby got the joints moving, and the back brake still held. I rode it up and down the gentle hills in the area; my motivation to keep going being the swarms of mosquitoes that bit me ferociously the moment I stopped or slowed down. I was exhausted in no time and had to wheel the bike up some of the hills. I promised to do this every morning. Get into shape for when Alice arrived at the end of the week. I was looking forward to her visit.

By midweek, I decided to crank up the old ride-on lawnmower. All it needed was some fuel, for the engine still ticked. I ran amuck over the grass that was threatening to take over the place. I wanted to restore *Water's Edge* to its splendour captured in the portrait hanging over the fireplace, a portrait created in the late 60s when house, water, manicured flower beds, and well-spaced cedars were stitched together with mown grass.

I made two discoveries during my clean-up. On a section of flat land by the western edge of the property, the lawnmower unravelled plastic marker lines nailed into the earth—the old tennis court where Margaret and her husband, presumably Grandpa Johnson, had spent many hours playing the game. In another section, which might have once been a flower bed, I found a cheap craft shop sign buried in the tall weeds: "One is nearer God's heart in a garden, than anywhere else on Earth."

I allowed myself a drink that night, to rest from my labours. The thought of the existence of Margaret's postcards intrigued me, and I couldn't resist looking for them before Alice got here. I searched all over: the bookcases in the house, the bedroom, the studio, the other nooks and crannies, the kitchen cabinets—nada!

The following morning, Alice called.

"Just thought I'd check in on how you are doing," she said.

I told her about my cottage restoration programme and my new keep-fit regimen.

"I'm impressed. You are on the road to recovery. My grandmother's home has been a good influence on you already."

"And you, too," I said. I heard her deep intake of breath.

"Why that's very nice of you. I'm surprised. You were always very scarce with compliments around the office, you know."

"I know. It's the corporate mantra we were raised with. 'Don't shit on your doorstep.'"

She giggled. "But now you are 'out of the house.'"

"That's right. And I can shit anywhere I wish."

"Thought you'd be glad to know that Higgins got canned yesterday. They walked him out. I was asked to help carry his things to the parking lot."

"Even gladiators of old got a nobler burial. They let him do all the dirty work getting rid of us minions then clobbered him. Serves the bastard right."

"Do you think they have an expiry date on me?"

"Every employee has an expiry date. You should start a business. Turn your grandmother's cottage into the resort she wanted. Be your own boss. I could work for you."

"It takes a special kind of courage to do that. I wish I was still that rebellious teenager. Somewhere along the way I got socialized. Made to subscribe to 'safe.'"

"Me too, kiddo. And now that I am unglued, it's pretty damned scary."

That night, I woke up from a nightmare. Nancy was on a bicycle chasing me while I was rowing furiously for the other shore, breathless and unable to get there in time before the giant tennis racket in her hand clobbered me senseless.

I flicked on the nightlight and lay awake until the vestiges of the dream had faded, finally chuckling nervously at its silliness. I realized I did not miss Nancy. I was not heartbroken, just relieved she had left. All the expectations we'd built our lives on had turned out to be vapourware, at least on my side. For her too, I guess—after I lost my paycheque. We had been two single people living with each other because we had been reluctant to find out what lay on the other shore. Well, she had at least moved onto her 'other shore', and I was still breathlessly attempting to find mine. I wasn't uneasy about Nancy's leaving, but I was scared about the Rump of Jim left behind. Who was I?

I looked at the photographs on the bedroom wall, shrouded in shadow. How must it have been for Margaret to start over each time with four husbands, in a bygone age when women were still relegated to domesticity? And yet she had done it. What had happened to Pope?

I shot up in bed. Why was I thinking about Pope? *Because he had been the first major turning point in her life. The first husband to meet his maker prematurely.* The first one is the hardest one, even murderers admit to it. I was going through my first wholesale life-change, and I wanted to know how Margaret had gone through hers. Pope, the photographer, was the wild card in her story that was otherwise portrayed so well on the wall, with the remaining holes filled in by Alice. I needed certainty, control, as my life was in freefall. I needed to understand this enigmatic centenarian and put her in her box. Classify her. Neutralize her. The postcards—I had to find them. They would reveal more about her life with Pope, I was sure.

The next day, I drove into town and bought a chicken, fresh vegetables, condiments, and some white wine even though Alice's visit was a couple of days away. Better to be prepared. I stopped in at the library and googled "Postcards in Canada." It appeared that postcards reached their high point in this country in 1914 when the cost of postage went from one cent to two cents due to the outbreak of war. Outrage followed, and postcard usage tailed off. Prior to the postal hike, however, postcards had been in fashion, the equivalent of e-mail today. Deliveries within the city were three times daily: people sent a postcard at 9 a.m. to be delivered by 12 noon to make an appointment for 4 p.m., all in the same day. Itinerant postcard makers— photographers on motorcycles—travelled the land taking pictures of landmarks and reproducing them in bulk for sale in gift and souvenir shops.

"Do you drink Chilean Chardonnay," I asked Alice when I called her that evening.

"Sure. That's sounds wonderful."

"How about Chicken Cordon Bleu?"

"Are you cooking already?" She stifled a chuckle.

"No, I was reading your grandmother's recipe book. She was quite the cook. She seemed to put her own spin on standard recipes."

"Grandma's Chicken Cordon Bleu was one of my favourites."

"Well, I will stick exactly to the recipe then."

Alice sighed, and her voice took on a reflective note. "That's the trouble with us, eh Jim? We stick to the knitting. Don't stray from the path; the side-roads are too dangerous."

I gulped. "Okay, I'll experiment then. I'll throw in some extra herbs. Perhaps some Indian spice as well. How about that?"

She laughed, a trifle hysterically. "Be crazy, Jim. Go wild! The office is too quiet these days. People are scared to say 'boo,' thinking they will get canned."

"And I'll ruin your grandmother's recipe. You won't mind?"

"But it will be your own. No, I won't mind."

The following morning, I took the canoe out again, determined to reach the other side. The speed boaters were strangely absent. Midway down the lake, the wind picked up. I kept paddling. My recent cycling up and down the Haliburton Highlands had improved my breathing. I was sure I could make it across. Then I heard a gurgling sound behind me. I felt beneath my feet, and the floor was wet. The canoe was taking in water at the stern. Before long, I was up to my ankles, just as I could make out Canadian flags at the cottages on the other side. A speedboat went by, and the driver cut his engine to reduce the wave effect on me. For once, I was glad to see one of them. The boater quickly assessed my predicament.

"Want some help?"

"I think I have sprung a leak."

He threw me a line. "Here, hang on, I'll tow you back."

In my anxiety to secure the line I forgot to mention to him that I wanted to get to the other side, not return from whence I had come. He pulled off with a roar and a jerk. I dropped my paddle overboard, and I could not shout out to him over the noise of the motor. We cut through the water in no time, and he deposited me safely on the dock of *Water's Edge*. He retrieved his line with a yank, waved, and took off again, leaving me back at square one with a leaky boat and no paddle.

After my ritual bicycle ride, I repaired the boat that afternoon. I was determined to make that opposite shore, come hell, high water, leaks, or missing paddles.

I found a piece of canvas in the shed and some superglue. The leak was in the seam so I plugged it well and good and laid the boat to dry upside down in the sun. I also raided the boathouse and found another paddle. Good, I was ready for my expedition the next day, in time to report to Alice that I had indeed taken my metaphoric challenge to explore new shores. I had already been having romantic day dreams of Alice and me running a thriving resort in this place as I had cycled the steep highlands of Haliburton.

As I was leaving the boathouse, I noticed a bookcase in one corner. It was partially covered with a burlap sheet. I moved the burlap aside and dusted the cobwebs from the case. Inside was a set of what I took to be encyclopaedias— all similar looking, hardbound, and numbered one to thirteen. Disappointed, I threw the cover back and went into the house as the sun went over the treeline. It was time to experiment with my cooking.

First, I fortified myself with three liberal fingers of scotch. I was nervous. More than nervous—a paralyzing fear had overcome me. My cooking attempts to date had been limited to opening tins and microwaving pre-cooked meals and the barbecue, of course. I'd cooked all my meals at the cottage so far on the barbecue. The scotch helped, and I needed several more fingers of the stuff before I could face that chicken. This time, the alcohol also brought out the pent-up resentment that had been hiding inside me all this time.

I looked up at Margaret's photograph in the kitchen, one taken in her 70s or 80s, when she had a look of satisfaction on her face as if she had achieved all her life's goals.

"Marge, don't look so smug up there," I said, twirling the whiskey in my glass. "You are no different from my Nancy—you married a string of meal tickets, that's how you scored. After your first husband died, you married the safe and stable schoolteacher. Then, when he passed on, you went up-market and married an hotelier. But he died before you could get your windfall, and you couldn't run that hotel by yourself. Oh yes, I saw the number of guests tail off in the final years in your registers. So, you sold out and married the insurance broker—set for life now, eh—with long-tail insurance commissions for many years to come. And I bet husband number four, jolly George Smith, must have insured his life for a fortune, being in the trade and all! Enough to start a resort in your hundreds, right?"

I was on a roll. I poured another drink and got down to my cooking.

And boy, did I experiment! With a vengeance. I ignored Margaret's recipe. I was envious of her. Or was it resentment? Was I mixing her up with my gold digger wife, Nancy? I browned the chicken then threw in parsley, rosemary, and thyme. Lots of salt followed, then pepper, some ginger topped up with *garam masala* which I had found surprisingly in this WASP town—maybe the immigrants were already creeping inland. Why not some alcohol to bring the dish to life? So, in went a liberal lacing of scotch. I needed gravy, so I made my own: milk, chicken stock, and curry leaves. I brought the whole thing to a boil and let it simmer. I realized I was really drunk when I drained the bottle of scotch to top up my empty glass. *Fear of stepping off the beaten path, Alice. You are so damned right!*

My Chicken-à-la-Jim tasted great—at that point of inebriation, shit would have tasted great—but it was no Cordon Bloody Bleu. I had ruined the recipe but transformed the chicken. I put the dish in the fridge to marinade. Let Alice taste my "experimentation" when she arrived tomorrow. She'd asked for it; she was going to get it.

Life on the edge ain't like anything you've tasted, honey!

I was determined as hell to find Margaret's secret recipe, the missing bit of her life with Pope, and expose her entire 102 years, cradle to grave, as one of privilege lived under the shelter of hardworking men, like me, who had propped up their women.

I searched everywhere, leaving a trail of strewn books, artifacts, photographs, and other odds and sods in my drunken wake. There would be a lot of cleaning up to do before Alice arrived tomorrow. But that was tomorrow. Today, I was on a mission.

Then it hit me—the boathouse! Why would someone leave a collection of elegant encyclopaedias in the boathouse? Unless that someone had not wanted nosey parkers like me to find something important in obvious places.

I staggered out onto the lawn. The wind was rising on the lake.

Inside the boathouse, I flung away the burlap and grabbed the first encyclopaedia.

It really wasn't an encyclopedia but a hardbound, outer cover that resembled one. It was a postcard album. And there were hundreds of postcards. From 1901 to 1914, and then they stopped. Because postage had doubled that year? A bundle of handwritten letters was loosely stuffed into the last album marked *1914*.

First, I read the letters; they were more recent and ran through assorted dates in the 1960s and 70s, all from various women friends, inviting Margaret to family get-togethers and picnics. One caught my attention; it was dated October 1978.

Dear Marge,

So sorry to hear about George's passing. Must have been such a surprise. Just after your Bermuda cruise and all. Men are such ignoramuses. Fancy not taking out a life policy when he worked in the business? Like my Wally, who was going to live forever... Ah but you have been there several times before, haven't you? Is this the fourth time for you? You must come to Ottawa next spring when the tulips are out....

Sarah

I dropped the letters and began with the albums, starting at the first year: 1901. I was quickly disappointed. Schoolgirl stuff. All about going to school during the week and to church on Sundays and how Tommy Dorsey's eyes were cute and Peter Phelps's acne was awful and the intricacy of the quilt her mother was knitting— yadda, yadda—girly stuff, further proof of the cosseted upbringing. I quickly jumped forward to 1907 when her life started to get a bit more interesting. Margaret was a nursing aide and debutante living in Toronto at that time and had various admirers, serious ones proposing marriage. And she was picky. One was by a wannabe on a card whose picture depicted a street scene of Oshawa before General Motors changed its face:

> *I am now working in a bakeshop in Oshawa. I remain your friend. R.V.*

Another, with a photograph of a stern young man wearing a monocle and dressed in a barrister's gown, read:

> *I did not go to the concert at Massey Hall in the end. I gave the tickets away. I will always remain your friend. A.W.*

The next was more aggressive: a picture of the Keewatin Docks on the front:

> *I never break my word. I asked. You refused. Farewell! P.D.*

What was up with these guys? Why the initials only? Afraid of something? No wonder she had told them all to take a hike!

Then I found Ernie Pope's postcards, beginning in 1909. They were his own creations, depicting street scenes of Toronto, the Don Valley, Ottawa, Kingston, Niagara

Falls; small towns with lighthouses and grain silos, Queens Park when it had gates, the Royal Alex theatre when it was a dour grey building, and one of the Empire State building in New York. The cards were branded Ernest Pope Souvenir Cards. His messages were light, one or two liners:

> *June 1909—Hope you are having a good time and the nursing is not too onerous. Off to Ottawa tomorrow— EP*
>
> *Nov 1909—In Kingston. The sun is shining despite the cold. Hope you are having a good time—Ernest*
>
> *Mar 1910—New York. This is the tallest building in the world. Hope to sell lots of copies—Ernie*
>
> *Sep 1910—Can't believe we are married a month. And here I am in Manitoba, still taking postcard pictures. Can't wait to hold you in my arms again—Ernie*

Ernie's last two cards in 1914 explained why the albums had ended:

> *Sep 1914—Having difficulty selling the last batch to the gift shops. Hope this war ends soon—Ernie*

And then:

> *Dec 1914—Honey, I can't beat this thing. The market is dead. I am enlisting. I have to—Ernie.*

Tucked into the plastic side flap of that album were two printed slips of paper. I fished them out.

The first read:

> *10 Sep 1916—His Majesty's Government regrets to inform you that your husband, Ernest Hargrove Pope, was lost in battle, presumed dead, in the Somme region of France. Please accept our condolences....*

The second was on the same government stationary, slightly newer paper:

10 Jul 1944—His Majesty's Government of Canada regrets to inform you that your spouse, Robert Armstrong Johnson, was killed in battle during the invasion of Normandy in France last month....

I had read enough. I rang Alice on my cell phone. She picked up sleepily.

"You didn't tell me your grandfather died in the war," I said.

"Well, you never asked. What are you doing at this time of the night?"

"I found the postcards. They were in the boathouse."

"I know. I could have told you that, too. You were supposed to wait until I got there to go over them with me. What's got into you? You sound... a bit crazed."

"I made a chicken recipe that is unreal. You won't want to miss it tomorrow."

"Er... Jim. About tomorrow..." Her voice had gone tense, and that made me pause. She took a deep breath and continued. "I was going to leave this for tomorrow, but I'd better tell you now."

"What? Have you decided to build that resort with me?"

"No. They offered me Higgins's job today. And I accepted."

"What!"

"Sorry, Jim. I am made for 'safe' only."

"But you were going to write Margaret's life story—"

"That will have to remain a work-in-progress for now. Do you still want me to come out tomorrow?"

I flung the phone away from me into the confines of the boathouse, shouting, "No, don't! Turncoat!" The cell phone hit the wall and went clattering away into the jumble of rusting equipment lying around.

I staggered back into the house, grabbed the chicken out the fridge, and chucked it into the garbage. I opened the two bottles of Chardonnay and poured the contents down the sink. I had never liked white wine anyway.

Margaret looked smugly down at me from the photograph.

I yelled at her. "In the end, we are all alone! That's how we make it, or break it—alone!" She didn't disagree with me.

I went outside again. A luminescent orange moon was rising over the trees. It lured me.

"Fuck you, Luce!"

I righted the repaired canoe and slid it into the water. Moonlight danced on the waves that were picking up from the rising wind, picking up swiftly now. There would be no speedboaters at this time of the night. I was going for that far shore, drunk as I was. When I pushed off, I realized I had not worn a life jacket, and my cell phone was back somewhere in the boat house.

"I'm sorry, Marge," was all I could say into the wind as I wrestled the paddle in the mounting waves, trying to develop a rhythm, trying to keep my heart rate even. "You never reached that shore, either. You were a work-in-progress all your life—the secret to your longevity."

I paddled and paddled through the night. Lucifer went behind a cloudbank, and all I could hear were his agents, those siren waves, slapping against the boat, sucking me in, while my paddle slapped them back. In the distance, lights peeped through the misty darkness on what must be the other shore. How far away was I? Would I reach it? My muscles screamed, and my heart felt like it would burst. I was a work-in-progress out there on that lake as the waves buffeted my puny canoe.

And that was the best way to be. Never complete unto the end. Always in motion... eh, Marge?

HER NEXT LIFE

Morgan walked into the master en-suite of the two-bedroom apartment she owned in downtown Toronto, a smart investment she had made after the divorce fifteen years ago, which she now owned outright. She couldn't afford to buy real estate in the city today. And very soon, if circumstances did not change, she would have to put this one up for rent and look for smaller digs.

Stripping, she appraised herself in the wardrobe mirror. Despite the boob-job ten years ago, her 36-D breasts sagged, but only a bit, and her stomach was still flat, although a slight roll was developing around her hips. Strong, long legs ended at a thin, Brazilian landing strip, which made her giggle—this had been a thing at the office among the women in her cohort. Apparently, everything was being shaved and shaped into designer styles—hair was out, hairless was in. The Brazilian made her contemporary, although it needed regular maintenance and made her feel like someone in Geraldine's set—still one had to do what it took to play in this new game. Her face was her strongest suit: large, brown eyes set symmetrically on either side of an aquiline nose and full lips above a strong jaw gave her the perfect combination of intelligence, femininity, and strength. She was getting used to the ash-blond hair dye, for it hid the grey, and today the roots needed touching up.

In her fifty-fifth year, Morgan Delaney had developed her next ten-year plan. Too old to get another executive job and too young to retire, she had figured out what she was going to do until RRSPs, government pension, and old-age security kicked in. Her elevator pitch: "If you can't make your wealth anymore, you marry it."

She ran a bath and luxuriated in it, exfoliating her face, shaving her underarms and legs and wondering what today's encounter would be like. After realizing that finding another career was going to be like seeking the proverbial needle, and in keeping with her "plan," Morgan had decided to find another man who would see her through to retirement and then some. Her requirements were precise: seventy or older, widowed or divorced, with assets that included a house; a man who was healthy and with no greedy children. The last requirement had been the hardest to meet, for most seventy-year-olds were not only fathers but grandfathers and great grandfathers. She never went to bed with the "candidate" until after the second date—the third date was too late for her and for her aging suitors, and her subscription to the dating site had an expiry date. If she did not like the man, she left before the bill came, pretending she had to powder her nose. Her membership with Big Fish in the Sea had just been extended for another six months, because the first subscription had yielded mainly encounters with liars, perverts, and impotent scoundrels.

As she soaked in the warm water, her mind went back to some of those past encounters. There had been the seventy-five-year-old pensioner with the stud farm who needed Viagra; he popped an extra pill just to prove his prowess and nearly had a heart attack on the first night they got into bed. The retired doctor had surprised her when he had given her a cane and asked her to spank him before they had sex. Then there was the Professor Emeritus with the cottage and the house in Forest Hill who had looked like a good catch. They had sailed through multiple dates and were planning a "surface only for meals" trip to Sandals in Jamaica over a candle-lit supper in Yorkville when his "dead wife" suddenly arrived and upset their plans by whacking the esteemed professor on the head several times with her handbag and driving him out of the restaurant while Morgan fled through another door.

She sighed as she slipped into fresh underwear and ran through the dresses in her closet, all bought when she had been V.P. of Administration during her last ten years at the firm, brand names that would set the right tone with the eligible and drive out the charlatans—well, at least that is what she hoped for, although the reality up to now had been somewhat different. She had felt powerful in those suits during board meetings and corporate events. That power had been stripped away when she received her severance package two years ago from the insurance company where she had worked for thirty years since graduating from university. And, in two more weeks, that package was ending.

She selected a burgundy and black dress with a bit of silver on it. Look dangerous but businesslike with Shawn—that was the name of her date tonight.

His photo had been taken against a backdrop of a large bookcase with weighty hard covers; he sported a grey moustache and goatee, manicured, and he had sensitive and intelligent eyes, a broad forehead, and a full head of steel-grey hair—not bad for a seventy-year-old. And he claimed to be a businessman dealing in antique works, and that meant money; like her, he was talking about making a start in a new direction, and he owned his apartment in downtown Toronto, above his store in the entertainment district. His hobbies were reading, writing book reviews and art essays, tennis, and hiking, so she concluded that he must be energetic, athletic, and hopefully, still virile! He was a recent widower after a thirty-five-year marriage. And he had no children. What a catch! And just in time too!

They met at a discreet Italian restaurant off King St. West, away from the big lights and noisy theatregoers lining up for mega-musicals on the strip, yet in a part of the city that smacked of life well-lived. He was just as his photo had presented him and Morgan was relieved—she had been through her quota of phonies who'd looked twenty years older on arrival. He had reserved a table by the window, illuminated by an elegant candle. He stood when she arrived and bowed, pushing her chair in after her. They ordered a bottle of Bordeaux while indulging in small talk, sizing each other up, silently verifying credentials and statements made in the flurry of e-mails that had flown by to set up this first date. From her standpoint, everything checked out, other than the quiet sadness that seemed to underlie his gentle conversation.

Over soup, they talked about their respective lives.

"My wife, Hilda, and I ran an antiquarian bookstore for over thirty years. We bought it soon after we married, for we both loved history, literature, and the fine arts."

Morgan swallowed. Her interest in reading had been limited to genre fiction and chick lit for the beach, and her magazine subscriptions to Maclean's and Vogue. Her life had been too busy and practical for diversions like serious literature. "You must have built up a large customer base in that time."

"Many have died. Quite a number don't read today, but we managed to hold it together."

"Do you still own the store?"

"Yes, the bookstore is my principal source of income. After Hilda died last year, the wind went out of it for me. She was my business manager, buying, selling, stocking, and dealing with suppliers and customers. I was the artistic director, if you will—I made the picks of what we got to buy and sell. Reading forgotten but rare books was a source of inspiration for me. And when a book sold and went from one hand to another—that was a tremendous encouragement."

I could be your business manager. I've run many departments in my career.

"And you never had children?" She had to be sure.

"Hilda was unable to conceive—that was her greatest sorrow. However, the bookstore was our baby that we nursed well into its adulthood."

Over a three-course dinner, she talked about her life, and he was an attentive listener. At one point, he surprised her by asking, "And what do you believe in?"

She choked on her meat and had to excuse herself. "You mean, as in 'religious belief'?"

"No." He looked embarrassed for asking the question and poured more wine into her glass. "I beg your pardon for the question."

"I'm not very religious, but I'm still a non-attending member of our local United Church."

"Ah." And he left it at that.

Over coffee, he talked about art and travel. He and Hilda had travelled to all six continents and spent a lot of time in Italy and France. Morgan had yet to visit those two destinations although she had made it as far as England once for a conference; she had preferred to spend her time taking junkets down south where it had been warm, just to escape the pressure of her work. She was captivated by the anecdotes he threw out about mad painters like Edward Munch and writers who died of drinking too much coffee, such as Balzac.

She placed her cup down, laughing. "I'd better not drink a second cup, then."

He laughed too. "Balzac drank fifty cups a day. I think you're safe."

She definitely wanted to meet this sad, learned man again. She felt she could complement him and replace his loss.

Just as they were settling their respective tabs, as was her custom on the first date, he said, "I would like to meet again. Would you come over to the shop?"

"Yes, that would be nice. I'd like that very much."

She could not get him out of her head for the rest of the week; his quiet dignity, his sadness, his knowledge without the taint of hubris. They had made an appointment for the coming Saturday, for a second date, to meet at his shop and go out for dinner afterwards. That was four days away, and the time didn't go quickly enough.

Geraldine, her offspring from a disastrous marriage to an alcoholic stockbroker, called on Friday evening. Geri worked as an art teacher in B.C., and rarely phoned, still upset about the family break up, although *she* had not had to face the shenanigans the drunken Brad doled out every night during those tumultuous final years following the market crash of '87. After the divorce, a teenage Geri had constantly sniped at Morgan and had preferred Brad's company, for "Daddy was, oh, so much cooler to be with." As for Brad, rudderless and jobless, he had driven his car into a tractor trailer while returning home from a boozy party ten years ago; luckily, Geri had not been with him.

"Did you hear of an antiquarian bookshop called The Vintage Menagerie when you were living in Toronto?" Morgan asked after they had gone through the pleasantries of health, weather, and had brought each other up to date on their daily travails.

"The one on King? I used to go there to research Greco-Roman art when the university library didn't stock the right books."

"Yes."

"Hmm." Morgan heard the clicking of keys at the other end. Her daughter never entered a conversation without Google by her side so that every unknown could be demystified. "It's rumoured here that they will be closing their doors soon. That's a shame. I loved that store. All of retail is in peril now."

"Closing? But that's impossible!" Morgan caught herself too late. And she kicked herself for not googling this information earlier—she had been busy daydreaming about her new Mr. Wonderful.

"What's your connection with the store?" Geri asked. "Don't tell me you're taking an interest in art now? You, who always insisted that I get a real job, like bean counting?"

"Now, now, let's not go there. We'll end up in another fight."

"Well, if you get down there before they close their doors, please give my regards to Mr. McGarry, I think his name was. Such a sweet man! And his wife."

"She's dead." Again, Morgan caught herself, again too late.

There was a long pause. "Mum, what's going on? Do you know these folks? Okay, I know. You're going to buy The Vintage Menagerie as part of your career remake and turn it into a Chapters franchise."

"Don't be silly. Are you sure they're closing? Shawn... Mr. McGarry... didn't tell me that."

A burst of laughter erupted at the other end, tinged with hysteria. Geri had always been intelligent but manic. "Oh, I see—you're dating Mr. McGarry!"

Geri had found out about Morgan's activities on Big Fish in the Sea after the Professor Emeritus affair had left her mother shaken. Morgan had blurted the whole thing out during one of their phone calls because she had not known whom to turn to.

Relieved that Gerri couldn't see her blush, Morgan said, "Well, we had a drink. And dinner."

"The plot thickens. And when are you going to sleep with him?"

"None of your business. How's *your* love life?"

"Dry as a desert. Perhaps I'll join Big Fish in the Sea."

"No way—then you'll be spending your time shadowing me rather than seeking your own Romeo."

"You're right. I think I'll focus on my work for now rather than on phony losers."

"Shawn is not a loser."

"Wonder why he chose to join that pathetic online bunch? Sorry, Mum, didn't mean to include you."

"Yes, you did. Well, anyway I have to go. Pizza's in the oven. I shall pass on your regards to Mr. McGarry."

I'll pass on more than regards to him, Morgan thought, as she put down the receiver. *He's got some explaining to do. Store closing!*

The store belonged to an earlier age; the gilt lettering of a classical font on its facade could have come from the roaring twenties. The inside was lined with heavy, dark, wood shelving that reached to the ceiling. The place smelled of old paper and spice. Every book was in its place. A quiet elegance emanated from the manner in which business was being conducted inside: Shawn, attending to an aged customer, was turning the pages of a large, leather-bound book and commenting on it while the customer nodded in rapt attention. Their sole focus was the book and its contents, and neither of them turned around when the bell on the front door tinkled to announce her arrival.

She waited for the customer to depart with his purchase wrapped in tissue and deposited in a gold logoed bag and distracted herself by browsing the shelves. Roman Art, the Great Literary Masters, Biographies of Musical Maestros, Plato's Thoughts—this was all a bit much for her. She knew without looking that she would not find her usual supply of John Grisham and *Fifty Shades.*

When the door finally closed behind the departing customer with the tinkle of the bell, and the cash register rang with finality, she burrowed deeper among the bookshelves, wondering when he would notice.

It did not take long, for he came rushing over to her, arms outstretched, a wide grin on his face. "Morgan! Sorry, I was tied up."

They embraced, and his goatee grazed her cheek. His eyes looked longingly at hers, and she hoped he would kiss her in the empty store, but he withdrew shyly. She straightened her coat, wondering if the hot feeling flowing through her was a blush or a hot flash.

"Nice place," she said, looking around the room. Then its flaws began to surface: the chipped plaster on a wall column, the crack in the window glass overlooking the street, the streak of dust on a nearby shelf that had missed the cleaner's brush, the fused bulb inside a fixture in the corner of the room.

"Yes, it's a hell of a job to maintain." He went over to the door and placed the "Closed" sign on it and locked it. "Let me show you around."

With the flair of a magician he took her around the shelves regaling her with tales of the French Revolution, pulling out an 1800's illustrated edition of Dante's Inferno, another of an original King James Bible covered in plastic wrap. The books got older the further the tour progressed; none from the big publishing houses she had heard of, all boutique creations. She stifled a yawn while trying to absorb the knowledge spilling out of Shawn, but his sheer energy and optimism kept her following his footsteps. He swelled in stature as he walked around.

"And now, to my office," he said. With pursed lips, he led her into a small room at the back. Books were piled everywhere, and a centre table was a mess of papers: bills, invoices, catalogues, pamphlets, cheque books, and newspaper clippings. Empty cartons were stacked in a corner. He pulled a chair out from behind a pile of books and offered her a seat while he went over to his table and perched on its edge.

"This is where I spend most of my time at night, on all the administrivia that Hilda took care of. I'm hopeless at it."

"Can't you hire someone?"

"I can't afford an assistant at this point." He shrugged and began pacing. He looked like a balloon from which the air had started to leak. "That customer you saw was the only one I've had the whole day. I could not lose him, even though I saw you enter from the corner of my eye."

"Is it true that you're going to close your doors?"

"The book business is an incestuous one. I see that you've been reading the gossip columns."

"It was my daughter, actually. She googled you. She sends her regards, by the way. Geri was a past customer of yours."

His eyes lit up again. "She remembers me! That's so rewarding. There are fewer and fewer customers who are loyal anymore. Original books do not have the value they once had. There are copies online everywhere."

"So, you *are* closing."

"Yes. But I'm also beginning elsewhere." With a sudden burst of energy, he went over to the door at the end of the room and threw it open, his hand outstretched theatrically, inviting her to follow him. "Where?"

"In cyberspace. If you can't beat 'em, join 'em, eh?"

"*You* are going to take on Amazon?"

He laughed hollowly. "Amazon does not have what I have. Come, let me show you the upstairs."

As she ascended the steps to his apartment, she felt as if she was being drawn deeper into his lair, and while she was allowing it to happen organically, her cautious, analytical self was saying to her that there were too many unanswered questions. Shawn was straying from her requirement. His sole asset had become a liability, and here he was talking about some scheme to compete with Amazon.

She hesitated before stepping into the apartment. He took her coat and hung it up. The presence of the other woman was strong. The collage of photographs in the foyer confirmed that: a young Shawn and a woman, who must be Hilda, on board a cruise ship, another on a sailboat, one of the couple taken in front of the Eiffel Tower, and another on a gondola in Venice. Morgan averted her gaze and stepped into the spacious living room where the walls were adorned with gilt-framed paintings. The crème lace curtains had a woman's touch—so did the pastel furniture. And there were fresh flowers in vases in several places. He took her around to the study, the spacious and neat kitchen, and threw the door open to the master bedroom.

She stood on the threshold of the bedroom and poked her head inside. A king-sized, four poster bed with the same pastel decor commanded the space, and an en-suite dressing room and bathroom ran off the side. A mahogany writing desk sat opposite the large windows that provided a glimpse of the lake through a freak break in the downtown concrete.

"I do a lot of my writing in this room," he said from behind her.

She shivered. She did not have writing in mind. She wanted to turn around impulsively and draw him over to that inviting bed but fought the thought.

She was relieved when they returned to the living room. He hurried over to the liquor cabinet. "Wine? How about a Shiraz? I have a good 1986 Australian, just for the occasion."

She clutched the drink and sank into the plush cushions on the sofa. The aroma and structure of the full-bodied vintage were excellent. Shawn had prepared well for this encounter. And the flowers, that had to be his touch. And yet, the flair and furnishings of the apartment did not correspond to a person surviving on one customer a day.

He had poured himself a double scotch, which was fast disappearing. He looked nervous as he took a seat in the lounge chair opposite her.

He followed her roving eyes around the room. "I know what you're thinking." He downed his drink and coughed. "I can't afford this. Well, not for long, anyway, if I continue like I have."

"What will you do when you sell the store?"

He rose and poured himself another drink, sipping this one slower than the first. Courage, assisted by the alcohol, was returning. She was starting to get her hackles up; memories of past unfortunate encounters with lonely old men started to rear their heads.

"The last time we met, I asked you what you believed in, and we did not quite get to the answer."

"I did not understand your question."

"It's about legacy. What do you care to leave behind when you die?"

"I haven't thought that far. I'm trying to get by each day."

"That's the problem—we do not see the wood for the trees."

"What do *you* believe in then?"

"Sharing this artistic wealth that I have hoarded with the world—that's what I believe in and have always believed in. For a long time, I thought this little store was the way to do that, but I was wrong. It was situated in too narrow a niche. Art is universal, and this is what these online retailers have taught me. So, I'm taking The Vintage Menagerie online. I have negotiated a deal with a reproducer and distributor of art books for the World Wide Web and we will establish an online catalogue, a shopping cart, and a subscription service. We will hold online exhibitions and go broad instead of deep. The distributor will handle that mess you saw in my back office."

"What about the competition? I'm sure others have done it."

"But my content is unique."

"When does all this start?

"Next month. The bookshop's premises are being leased to a clothing store, and I will announce a clearance sale next week. Certain items will be retained for online reproduction, some are being donated to museums, and the rest will be given away at fire-sale prices."

"It seems like you have found your niche."

"No—it is the biggest risk in my life. I've mortgaged the apartment for this. And I need someone to share the thrill ride with."

Her fingers started to get clammy, and she gulped her wine.

Suddenly, he was sprawled before her feet, taking the wine glass from her, placing it on the side table and taking her hands in his. "Dear Morgan, are you that person? I'm not asking for money; I'm asking for belief."

This time it had to be a hot flash for she must have gone a deep crimson, and he looked alarmed. "Have I shocked you?"

"No... no... this is so sudden. How can I *believe* when the things I gave myself to, a husband and a corporation, *both* let me down? When everything I have explored since, from consulting to franchising, is just consumerist vapourware? Besides, this is only our second date."

"Yes, yes, I know. This is when we were supposed to go to bed, right? But I cannot do that until I know whether you can stand shoulder to shoulder with me on this momentous leap in my life." He ran his hands through his hair, tousling it.

"And if I don't? Will you still leap?"

"I have no choice. My life has brought me to this pass."

She stood up and swayed over to the windows. Crowds hurried along King Street. She wanted to melt in with them, dissolve from this room. "You are seventy-years-old, Shawn. And you're trying to start again, in a very high-risk venture."

"I'm starting with what my heart is telling me is right and what the art of survival is telling me is my only way out. At some point in your life, you have to make these leaps."

She turned and faced her dilemma. With his dishevelled hair and flushed face, his age was showing; a man who had all the traits of a companion she would enjoy very much, and yet who was acting like a poker player in Vegas.

"I'd like to go home and think about it," she said, staggering towards the coat cupboard.

As she flowed with the crowds of theatre goers, tourists, and thrill seekers along King Street, heading for the streetcar that would take her home, she realized she wouldn't be going out on another date with Shawn. He had failed her criteria. And she had failed his. And he didn't look like a man who would be stirred by a Brazilian cut, or a Greek, for that matter.

What bothered her most was the question he had asked, "What do you believe in?" Right now, at fifty-five years of age, despite her grand ten-year plan, she did not know the answer.

FOUNDLING

I saw her at my wife's funeral.

She was giving Brad a hug. I kept staring at her like a man overboard, clutching desperately to the lifeline that would return him to the land of the living. Julie and I had been married for 30 years, and I'd just lost more than half of my life with her untimely exit; the future was a scary blob. The hipflask was burning a hole in my pocket, but this was no place to take a swig.

She stared at me across the funeral parlour, where friends and family were gathered in clumps. No one paid me much attention. After all, I was the non-entity in the family, the occasional teacher and house-husband who had written a few novels, one of which had hit literary stardom fifteen years ago and plunged me into a drought afterwards, from which I had never emerged.

Brad, Julie's and my only child, a 28-year-old up-and-comer on Bay Street, clapped me on the back. "Come on, Dad. Off with the mournful look. Mom would not have wanted to see you like this."

"Your mum was closing her last real estate deal on her deathbed," I reminded him.

His features slipped. Brad had not quite learned to keep a poker face like his mother had, even when she was diagnosed. Despite being his mum's protégé, he still had some learning to do if he was going to swim with the sharks on the Street and not be devoured.

"I'll be all right. This is just another milestone. I didn't think it would come so soon, though," I said.

"You can retire now and write those books that have eluded you. Mom's insurance has left you well off." Like his mother, Brad first covered the financial bases. This conversation did not excite me.

"There is someone I have to meet," I said, moving away. "The lady who was with you a little while ago—an old friend."

He looked in her direction with a puzzled frown. "Yes, there was something about her that was familiar, but I could not put my finger on it. She seems very nice."

I left him to do the mingling and headed over for a meeting with history.

The woman was engaged in the slide display of Julie's life flashing across the TV monitor in an alcove of the reception room. "A celebration of life" they called it these days, not the mourning of death as we had come to learn it in the old country. In the shadow of the alcove, I paused for a quick guzzle from the flask. Wiping my mouth, I moved in on her.

She turned as I neared, and her brown eyes stared right into mine, making my knees buckle. She had aged well: still the voluptuous mouth, the full-bodied figure. The whiskey tingled through me, and I felt guilty. She had been a teetotaller, I recalled.

"Valerie?"

"Tony." Her embrace was warm. We were reaching across a chasm. And yet there was tentativeness, as if she was searching for what was real in me. A fiction writer—what was real in us who hid behind other people's stories?

In embarrassment, and to hide my whiskey breath, I broke off our embrace prematurely and turned away to stare at the monitor. She did the same, her sleeve touching mine. There were scenes of multiple vacations—Julie had to get away every three months to escape the pace of her work, even though she thrived on it. Pictures aboard cruise ships, under palm trees, and against golden sunsets, and wearing Mickey Mouse costumes, slides of Brad playing hockey and baseball and of his university graduation and bar admission. Julie looked thinner in the last photograph. I should have suspected something and asked her to slow down.

"She was a beautiful and energetic woman," Valerie said.

"A life force went out of me," I said.

"It's awkward meeting under these circumstances. Brad's a nice boy. He looks a lot like you."

"Thanks for locating me on Facebook. I couldn't have taken the shock of seeing you after all these years without advance notice."

"You are easier to find because you put yourself out there. I am more private."

"My publisher expects me to build 'my platform' these days. So, I have become a literary prostitute, and I hate it."

"'Just google me,' eh?"

"It still does not sell books."

"Famous but poor?"

"The opposite. I am supposed to be well-off now, thanks to Julie. Yet, fame is an illusion—here today, gone tomorrow. Like happiness."

"We were happy, once..."

Brad came charging over to say the mayor was leaving and could I go and thank His Worship for taking time out of his busy schedule to pay his respects.

I caught only glimpses of Valerie after that, in-between shaking hands and accepting shallow condolences from people I hardly knew. Once I saw her talking to Brad again, exchanging cards, and giving him another hug. When I finally broke away from the condolers, she was gone.

I met Valerie again, two weeks later, pre-arranged this time via Facebook. We met at Christakos', a grill on the Danforth. She was reading a menu at a table by the window when I dashed in; I was harried by the traffic, intimidated from driving in Julie's SUV—who was I trying to impress—and fearing Valerie had already left.

"Sorry. It's mayhem on the streets at this hour."

She laid the menu down and smiled. "I walked."

She had let her hair down, dark ringlets falling over her shoulders, complementing her hazel eyes. Her hair has been dyed, I convinced myself. The nurse's uniform straight-jacketed her curvaceous body.

"Thanks for agreeing to see me on your dinner break," I opened. "Shift-work must be draining."

"You get used to it. Like you get used to many things in life."

"Didn't know you were at St. Thomas's. Brad was born there."

"Been there since I graduated. Sorry, I missed Brad's arrival. I must have been on maternity leave myself at the time. After meeting him at Julie's funeral, Brad has become a friend of mine on Facebook. That's a good start I guess, to get to know him." We talked about Brad. She seemed hungry for news about my upwardly mobile son.

We ordered, chicken souvlaki for me and a Greek salad for her. She naturally declined wine, but I ordered a bottle of Retsina anyway.

"I am a vegetarian now," she explained.

"I remember the rare steaks we'd guzzle in Cabbagetown, the times when we had money." I wanted to dive into the important parts of our lives, but here I was skirting around with inane musings about food. I wanted to reminisce about those early days when we were newly arrived off the boat and experimenting with Canada's multi-faceted cuisine, culture, and geography, not sure whose career would take off before the other's and in which direction. I wanted to ask her what had happened after our split.

Her hand rested on mine, sending shock waves down my spine. Her look was direct. "How are you settling into being on your own, a widower?"

"Fine," I said. Then I changed my mind. "Not fine, really. I drink a lot now that Brad has returned to his condo and his girlfriend. He must have told you that by now via Facebook." The wine arrived. I poured myself a glass and downed half of it in a gulp.

"You always drank," she said.

"My tolerance for alcohol has expanded. I've never been this... desolate."

"Now you know what it feels like to lose someone."

I ignored the iciness that had crept into her tone and focussed on my drink. "I'm not used to living on my own. I've always had a woman in my life. After my mother, there was you and then Julie. No time for a man to do his own cooking, clean his house. I'm playing catch up. Look, I'm sorry I didn't ask before, but, are you married?"

"No, never was. I embraced nursing after you left. Relationships only end in heartache."

I did not know what to say. She was boxing me into a corner each time, leaving me struggling for a new line in our conversation. Was she trying to hurt me after all these years? Was she enjoying watching me squirm?

"No relationships whatsoever? But you mentioned a maternity leave."

"Sperm bank. But I had to give him up for adoption— my hospital shifts and single motherhood did not work out. Tom tracked me down via Facebook recently. He is doing odd jobs out in the Alberta tar sands. Didn't make good life choices like Brad. Didn't have the connections or the education."

I let this sink in. "Hmm. Do you know who Tom's biological father is?"

"Sure. I picked his sperm from the range on offer at the bank. He is a famous author."

A tic started in my temple. I remembered how desperate living with Valerie had been, when she was studying for her nursing diploma and I was doing odd jobs to pay the bills. Our little bug-infested apartment in East York. Those frequent visits to that clinic on Davenport Road where they gave you a porn magazine and a vial and sent you into a cubicle. I had returned many times after the first awkward visit. And I had taken Valerie for those steaks on Parliament Street after every paid ejaculation— the only time I had a bit of extra cash. *Did she ever find out?*

"Need I ask this author's name? I'm jealous."

She pursed her lips and looked at the waiter who was arriving with our food. "I had to replace you quickly, and I did. I followed your exploits from a distance." She looked at her watch. "Unfortunately, I have to eat and go. I only have an hour for my dinner break. And I don't get off until midnight."

I drank more while we ate. I was a poor eater. I'd lost my appetite ever since my book went off the best-seller list those many years ago. The anxiety of trying for a sophomore hit had eaten away at my stomach lining, I guess. I could only tolerate alcohol. I watched her eat, in her methodical way, chewing her food carefully, leaving no leftovers on the plate, a conditioning from the old country where food had always been in short supply. I talked while she ate, about the rejection letters and the letdown after the blockbuster, and the writer's block that plagued me like a chronic disease. I sensed that the more I talked the less I impressed her.

"I know you'll never forgive me for leaving," I said, nibbling the chicken cubes on my skewer.

She sighed, as if expecting this moment to come. She pushed her plate away. She took a drink of water and wiped her mouth with her napkin. "You were looking for a sustainable life, for a writer's patron. I was a liability. You ran."

"I'm sorry."

"I've always wanted to ask you where you met Julie. And when. The farewell note you left on the dining table for me that night when I returned from nursing school was not very descriptive."

I decided not to elaborate on my way of ending relationships, even one as long as ours that had spanned two countries. Instead, I went on to describe events more positively. "I was tired of scraping to get by. One day, in a fit of delusion, I walked into a high-end realty office in Yorkville and pretended that I wanted to buy a property in Forest Hill. Seven hundred and fifty Gs, back in those days. I wanted to feel what it would be like when I had my first best-seller. Julie was the real-estate agent who took me house-hunting."

"You did this while I was at school? Like those visits to the sperm bank—those were before you met Julie, I presume? What else didn't you tell me?"

I put my chicken skewer down and filled my glass again. I had been an idiot to think I could have concealed things from a woman who slept in the same bed with me at night. "Julie saw my romantic side and believed in me. Unlike you, always telling me to give up my dream and get a real job." I wanted to hurt her, too, now that she had me against the ropes.

"You still do not have a real job."

"But I managed a best-seller. Though it was not enough to buy that house in Forest Hill. It doesn't matter now. I've inherited Julie's family home, and it's only a block away from the Hill."

"You saw a good deal in Julie, and you grabbed it."

I drained my glass. The bottle was empty. I signalled the waiter for another as Valerie wrinkled her nose. "Sometimes the only way to end a relationship is to do it abruptly. I am sorry."

"I have to go," she said pulling cash out of her handbag. "I can't wait and watch you finish the next bottle."

"Oh, don't worry about the bill," I said. "This is my treat."

"I've always paid my way." She placed a twenty on the table. The iciness had returned, and the brown pools in her eyes had solidified into stone. "There is something I want to show you before I leave."

She fished inside her bag and came out with a photograph. It was of a man in his late twenties. I gasped. I was looking at the spitting image of me, down to the dreamy eyes and curly black hair.

"Your son," she said. "The one doing odd jobs in Alberta."

My addled brain was trying to make connections. "I don't get it... *mine?*"

"Yes, yours." She pushed her chair back. "Goodbye, Tony. I came here under the illusion that there might be a life together for us, now that Julie has passed. But there is no road back. We have *both* hurt each other too much." She gathered her purse and ran out of the restaurant.

Dazed, I pulled my wallet out, removed the picture I carried of Brad, and placed it next to the one of the boy, Tom, from Alberta. My features in both men were dominant.

Then their maternal sides. Something that could only become evident upon seeing Tom's photograph and meeting Valerie after all these years began to bubble to the surface, and I started to sweat the alcohol out of me. I reached for the bottle.

<hr>

I drank a lot that evening at Christakos', letting the image of Valerie and her actions that had led to this pass fill the blanks in my mind as the alcohol slowly dulled my pain. Like plotting a novel, I retraced her steps to the hospital, not today as she returned to complete her shift, but on that other day 28 years ago when she carried a newborn—the child Julie and I would learn to call Brad— into the hospital. Brad, the egg of Valerie, fertilized into life by one of my multiple ejaculations reposing in a test tube at the clinic on Davenport Road.

She had brought the infant in for a "show and tell," at least that is what she must have told the nurses on her floor who were expecting her. Her stalking of me—"I followed your exploits from a distance"—since our split-up had also revealed that my wife had just given birth to a baby boy who was in the nursery. She badged-in at the entrance, waved to the security guard, and made for an empty elevator. Ever since hearing the news of our baby, her curiosity to see this other life that I had begat with Julie had been overpowering. Instead of going up to her floor, she stopped off on the second and went directly to the nursery. The nurse on duty, who faintly recognized her, nodded, but was busy with some charts on her desk. Locating Julie's and my son from among the row of bassinets, the child Valerie had called Tom but was labelled Brad on the hospital card, was easy.

"Look at him, darling," she whispered to the infant in the pouch strapped to her waist. "Your brother. He looks exactly like you. He will have all the privilege that you will be denied. Isn't he beautiful?" Something snapped inside her, and the desperate, impulsive, and needy purpose of having embedded my cryogenic sperm inside her became diabolically clear. "I'll teach that slimy father of yours for abandoning us."

She looked around. There was no one in the nursery other than the duty nurse who was still poring over her papers. Valerie uncovered the slumbering child snuggled in her warmth, and placed Brad next to Tom. *One of you must pay for your father's treachery, and the other will reap his just reward.*

She removed Tom from his cozy cradle and placed him inside her pouch. The nurse had not looked up once during the exchange.

Valerie left the nursery and went upstairs triumphantly for her "show and tell."

There are many plots that a novelist conjures in the course of his work, discarding each when implausibility renders it unusable. Perhaps there is another version of this story, the true one. But as I drained the bottle and ordered a third, and figured I would be going home in a taxi, I settled on this ending. This was one plot I was never going to be able to write about, and one which I would have to live with forever. Pity, for it could have been my sophomore best-seller.

FILLER

I maneuvered my groaning Honda through crawling traffic on the Parkway, looking for deliverance from this metal and exhaust fume parade that lurched daily in and out of the city. Aunt Tilda's words from yesterday reverberated: "You need a *real* job. Real estate—that's where it's at. Look at those towers." I could see them over the Don Valley, sticking their concrete blocks and construction cranes into the sky, changing this once dour city into a global property speculation bubble. The towers were all she could see from her hospital bed at Princess Margaret's, where she was going downhill rapidly. Dear Aunt Tilda. My only relative since my parents and their car went under a tractor-trailer on this same highway ten years ago; the dear spinster who had seen me through high school and university and had always worried about my future. Getting up in the mornings to the prospect of the grand dame's demise was difficult. Today had been one of those days.

I was going to be late, so I cut in front of an SUV to take the Don Mills Road exit and traverse side roads to Rosedale. My editor, Bob, had been very clear. "Maureen Fisher will see you at exactly nine o'clock. She doesn't tolerate lateness. As for the other fella—you get to him when able. He's just filler."

The Honda chugged uphill. It needed a new muffler, and I had been too proud to ask Aunt Tilda for a "loan" now that I was all grown up. As Canada's most stolen car model, I wondered why the old clunker did not get pinched and leave me free to collect on insurance.

I hated my job as a journalist at this magazine that had started out literary and had morphed into a celebrity gossip rag. "You gotta give them what they want," Bob had explained. "Tastes are a-changing in this social media world. It's all about bites, Niles, sound bites."

I wanted to write my own novel, not these chatty pieces, but I had to keep the wolf from the door, and this was all that an arts graduate with a lit major could get these days if he did not want to become a supply teacher on temporary wages and no benefits.

Maureen Fisher was difficult, I had been warned, and yet she was the darling of our literary world, having won every major award there was to win, barring the Nobel, which I was told was also in the cards when it next came around to Canada's turn. She was news; every time she opened her mouth, books flew off retail shelves and into readers' shopping carts. Bob had worked for months to get this interview and had decided to send me at the last minute, in case he screwed things up. He wouldn't admit it, of course, instead he had said, "Your career is riding on this one, Niles."

I pulled up outside the giant Casa Loma-like, three-story mansion on a tree-lined street with other mansions. After some consideration, I drove my rust bucket to the end of the cul-de-sac and walked back, in case Maureen was looking through the window and decided she did not want to talk to such a decrepit journal whose staff drove safety hazards.

The huge oak door, sporting a keyhole that ended at the nib of the bas relief of a quill, swung open. A bored matron dressed in a starched white blouse, blue skirt, and pumps looked at me through hooded eyes. "You're late, Mr. Niles."

"Traffic," I offered and decided to remove my shoes before I brought Toronto's construction dirt onto the thick beige carpet. The major domo wrinkled her nose at my socks—I admit I had been in them a couple of days and should have thought to wear fresh ones, if I could find any without holes in them, that is. She opened a coat closet and pulled out a pair of house slippers. "Put these on."

I followed her down a hall adorned with period oil paintings, Ming vases, and fresh flowers and turned the corner into a study lined with book cases filled with hard covers smelling of ripening paper. When the double doors clicked shut behind me, I recognized the woman standing by the ceiling-to-floor windows at the far corner, a book in her hand, reminiscent of an ice maiden before the spring thaw, looking out at those towers that seemed nearer from here.

In profile, her aquiline nose was her most prominent feature. Her hair was dyed red and held back with a scarf. The gold gown and the shimmering silver-heeled stilettos did not hide the fact that Maureen Fisher was shorter and more wrinkled than in the photographs I had seen of her. I felt as if I was a member of the crowd cast on a movie set.

She snapped out of her freeze and came towards me with surprising agility. "Sit down. You're late. I have exactly thirty-two minutes before my next phone call. With the *New York Times*."

I sat at the lower end, the foot-side, of a 19th century chaise lounge she waived me towards. She positioned herself in the Victorian armchair opposite, blocking out the sunlight, crossing her legs and striking a pose.

She tossed the book in her hand onto the coffee table between us. Waves of heavy perfume escaped with her movements. "I asked your boss to talk to me about my latest release in this interview. We need hype and positioning. It's a departure from what I have done before."

I took out my notes of pre-agreed questions between Bob and Maureen's agent and stared at them. None of them made sense. They were unsubtle cues to launch Maureen into waves of self-glorification. So, I asked her one of my own instead. "You have written on many themes: small-town intrigues, dysfunctional families, coming of age, dystopias, and so on. Have you experienced any of these situations first hand?"

"A writer needs research and imagination. Not everything has to be experienced."

"Is your last theme, the vampire feminist, tapped out?"

Her mask of control dropped momentarily. She squinted as if trying to recall where in the script her stupid agent had slipped in these questions, then replied brusquely, "That's not a question I can answer, but here's what I can tell you..." whereupon she bridged into her experiences with writing this new book, a supernatural thriller, rendered in literary style. Her explanation lasted 15 minutes and was littered with the names of celebrities and experts she had consulted, the moments of self-doubt, the discussions with her editor and agent, and she ended with, "...this genre needs gentrifying and respectability."

"Areyoulookingatthisnewmedium,onepeopledmostly by young readers, as a way of extending your shelf-life as a writer?"

She scowled. "Writers evolve. I see lots of scope in supernatural literary thrillers. My job is to extend the boundaries of the genre so generations of writers who follow me will mine new areas within it."

"I'm told that your book has already been nominated for every major literary award. Your agent must be busy; the book has only been out a week."

Her smile was glassy. "I have good people watching out for me."

"Is it important for you to win prizes? They sell books, I know."

"That is for the juries and my readers to decide."

"Aren't you willing to concede the podium to younger writers, now that you have won every conceivable award out there?"

"I consider myself a mentor and guide in the literary field, having been at it for over forty years. When I started, there was no Canadian literature to speak of."

"But now you have cornered the market and shut everyone out. When you retire, or die, there will be a hole in Canadian literature again. How do you reconcile this game of creating barriers to entry?"

She stood to her full height of five feet two inches. "Are you recording this?"

"I have only my handwritten notes. I do not carry tape recorders."

"Who the devil sent you here?"

"I believe in candid interviews. David Frost made his reputation on them."

"And you will get fired for them, young man."

"Not in the age of social media."

She stalked over to her desk, a monstrous mahogany affair bigger than my old Honda. Picking up the phone, she barked, "Hilda, show this gentleman out, and get me my New York call."

I put my notebook away in my satchel. "Thanks for the slippers. They are very comfortable."

Maureen Fisher was already poring over some papers on her desk, her fingers twitching by the phone that would ring from a more agreeable and accommodating journalist, perhaps one who would continue to propagate her mystique and flagellate himself before her fame.

When the front door slammed behind me—extra hard, I thought—I wondered what had gotten into me. I guess it was Aunt Tilda.

I got into my car and phoned the hospital. The nurse on duty said my aunt was stable, but they could not rule out a relapse, so she was being monitored. I wanted to forget about work, drive to St. Margaret's, sit beside Aunt Tilda, and provide her the companionship she had lacked all her life as a career schoolteacher who had given her all to her students but had never received much in return.

Then I remembered the other interview, the filler, as Bob had called it. Some obscure writer who would be the foil to Maureen Fisher in my article. This other interview was only going to delay me, but I liked to finish what I started, and I always did my best. That's why Bob grudgingly acknowledged me as his most competent, though thoroughly un-ambitious, journalist. As I drove back along the Don Valley Parkway, it struck me that you could only see the mountain when down in the valley, and I was driving to interview the "valley" of my article. I promised myself to make it quick; then I would take the rest of the day off and spend it with my dying aunt.

His name was Gustav Schmidt, according to his bio, and he lived in a crumbling apartment building on the eastern edge of the city, an area that would soon make way for expensive condos; the re-zoning signs were posted everywhere. The walkway to his four-storey brown brick apartment was littered with empty pop bottles, brown paper bags, and the odd used condom. I had difficulty locating his buzzer. I tried "Gus Smith."

"Come in," a raspy voice answered.

The single elevator was out of commission, but I didn't need it as I had to take the stairs down to the basement level.

Two cats peeked their heads out of his door, which opened fully to reveal a gaunt man well over six feet, stooped, dressed in a flowing caftan and a peaked cloth hat. The long grey beard that reached down to his chest was his most striking feature, next to his piercing black eyes. I thought I was in the presence of a wizard.

"I was about to take the cats for a walk," he said, ushering me inside by waving his walking stick. "I didn't think you would come."

His voice had no trace of the German accent his name had suggested. He was too young to have fought in the war, I figured. He coughed behind me, a wheezy cough.

The living room of the apartment was packed with books, in piles on the floor, over the scarred writing desk, and on the faded sofa. A monstrous desktop computer of a bygone era fought for space with the printed matter on the desk. A rectangle of daylight filtered in from a high window just below the ceiling through which I saw people's feet walking by; occasionally a carelessly discarded cigarette butt or pop can hit the glass and stayed lodged against it. There were no tall towers to be seen through that window, thank God!

He moved some of the tomes from the sofa to the floor, raising small clouds of dust that made him cough again. He bade me to sit. The cats sniffed around me and lost interest, disappearing somewhere among the columns of literature. Gustav went behind his writing desk and rolled out a chair. He removed his hat, allowing a roll of curly grey hair to fall across his shoulders.

I did not need notes for this interview. Bob hadn't given me any.

"You speak as if you have been let down by our journal in the past. By journalists in general."

"They always say that they will come, but they never do."

"I haven't heard of your books. How many have you published?"

"Self-published." Then he chuckled. "No publisher will stick his name behind me."

I wondered how Bob had got wind of this guy. Perhaps self-publishing was slowly creeping into respectability these days.

"Can you show me some of your books? I confess, I've had no advance information on you or your work."

"See that shelf?" He pointed a bony hand towards a bookshelf at the far end. It had the most uncluttered row of books in the room, about a dozen obscure titles. "Those are all mine."

I strained my eyes to read the spines, then gave up and asked him, "Perhaps, you'd like to tell me about them. From the beginning..."

"My parents came here after the last war. I was four. We were on the wrong side of history, the bad guys. Nazis, they called us."

"Did your father fight in the war?"

"He drove an ambulance in Germany. He saved lives. He tried to do the same thing here, but they wouldn't hire him. So, he went to the mines and sent money home. Until a mine collapsed on him."

"I'm sorry to hear that."

"Don't kid me. No one is really sorry."

"Your books. Tell me about those."

"My first book was about integration. I was tired of being labelled. When I was growing up in this country you were a Nazi, a Jew, a Dago, or a Frog, or whatever stamp you carried from the home country you had fled. I wrote about a utopian time when everyone would throw down their turbans, crucifixes, feathers, and kippas and wear tuques instead."

"That did not go down well, I take it."

"My sequel was more controversial. I proposed that everyone in this land had to have only one passport, a Canadian one. Those refusing, especially those permanent residents who kept their feet in two camps until they died, were to be deported."

"This makes Canada another type of Nazi society."

"A gentler, more rational one, I thought. You are either in or out. New worlds must learn from the previous ones and never make those past mistakes. We came here because Germany failed to live up to its promise and became something sinister. What I saw here was a tolerance for every bad influence in the world with this 'multi-culturalism' business we keep hanging onto. Fundamentalism has taken root as a result, you know."

I realized I had left my cell phone in the car and was therefore anxious to push this interview along. However, Gustav was provoking my curiosity. "What else have you written?"

"Oh, in separate books, I took on the right wing, the left wing, the religious establishment, the corporate establishment, our entitlement society. I ran into trouble when I took on the radical branch of the feminists."

"What happened there?"

"Oh, I created a mythical matriarchal world in which women did the brain work and men the grunt work. Then that world fell apart when greed took over. Men *or women*, we are all susceptible to greed."

Remembering my recent interview with Maureen, I chuckled. "I bet *that* did not go over well."

"My manuscript was turned down by every publisher I sent it to. When I finally self-published it, I received hate mail from the few readers who picked up the book."

"You certainly did not make friends. How did you sell your books?"

"Oh, I would turn up at craft shows and farmer's markets. Sell a few books here, a few books there. I gave a lot of them away for free by standing at street corners. It's funny how people like 'free' and will stretch their hands out not knowing what the heck they are receiving. Most of my hate mail came from those freebie lovers, I think."

He had to stop at that point for his coughing had returned, stronger, making him double up. "My lungs," he gasped. "Worked in a factory once. Life was never the same afterwards." He fished out a puffer from his pocket and took several inhalations, and we remained silent until he regained his breath.

"My aunt has weak lungs too," I said. "It's landed her in hospital this time."

"It gets you in the end."

I quickly changed the subject, and we talked more, and I forgot the time. He told me about his younger days in Toronto, struggling to make it in academia where his anti-establishment views would always get him into trouble; his drift into journalism only to find more 'in-the-box' writing; a job as political activist for a major provincial party followed until he discovered that the party's marching orders came from corporate sponsors.

"I joined the priesthood. Then Mount Cashel blew up in our faces, and I realized that one had to be a saint or a pervert to be in that business, and I was neither, so I left."

A string of odd jobs had followed ending in a security guard position, until retirement mercifully delivered him to live a sparse life, dedicated to writing in this subterranean apartment with his cats for company. He had never married and never had any children.

"I'm sorry that our literary establishment ignored you," I said.

"That was a bit of good fortune. I want to write from the outside, as the observer. Groups expect conformity." There was a hint of defiance in his voice.

"I've been thinking of writing my own book," I ventured. This was the first time I had spoken about this intention to anyone. I had not even told Aunt Tilda. "I want to write about my chronically overeducated and under-employed generation."

"A worthy topic. But you can't just *think* about it. If you believe, you must commit."

He rose, went over to his private collection, and picked up a book. He handed it to me. "This is my gift to you. I hope you read it."

The book had no fancy cover, just a plain white background with bold black lettering that said *Greed*. There wasn't an author's name on the front. I flipped through the pages, and the writing came across as intelligent without belligerence. I was curious to read it the moment I got home.

He continued whimsically, "My next book will be on the famine of time. Whenever I write something, I realize that I will be asking, nay—stealing—someone's time to read it. And with all the non-essential things we need in our lives today, we have no more time. My protagonist has discovered how to bend time and has invented the twenty-seven-hour day, and everyone is after him because it is the new gold."

I closed my notepad and put it, along with Gustav's book, in my bag. I was reluctant to leave. "You should have a lot of fun writing about the 'famine'—it's a pandemic. I'm afflicted too, for I have to go. I have another appointment."

He took my hand in a warm handshake. "Thank you for coming. And thank your boss for responding to my letter."

I did not want to tell him the real reason for my boss's acquiescence but promised to come again and have a more informal chat, off the record, once I had finished reading his book.

His dark eyes glistened, and for the first time I saw him smile. "That, indeed, would be wonderful. I do not have much company." The cats appeared as if on cue, and he picked them up, one in each arm. "Except for my kitties."

There was a voice message on my cell phone when I got to the car. "...sorry to advise you Mr. Niles... your aunt took a sudden turn for the worse..." She was gone. In that moment, the image of Gustav Schmidt flashed in place of my dead aunt—don't ask me why.

"Niles—what the hell!"

I'd figured Bob was going to blow his top when I turned in my story. He had generously given me a week to do so, as I'd had to attend to Aunt Tilda's funeral and financial affairs. That time away had hardened my resolve about how I was going to spend the rest of my life.

"Don't you get it, Niles? The old geezer was the filler." I thought Bob was going to have a coronary, he was screaming hoarsely at the other end of the phone.

"He wasn't—not in my view. He had the better story."

"And comments like 'Fisher is an insecure writer, clinging to her fragile perch'—where the heck did that come from?"

"It's true. And the truth hurts." I recalled Gustav's words and added, "...and rarely ever gets published."

"You're fired, Niles."

"Thanks, Bob. That saves me from writing a letter of resignation."

I heard papers ripping in the background. "This story is toast. Do you hear, Niles? Toast!"

"It's not, Bob. I posted it on all the citizen newspapers an hour ago. Facebook and Twitter have picked it up, and

I think it's going viral as we speak. You should check into social media more often."

I put down the phone before any more apoplectic invective came through.

I looked out at the distant downtown towers from my apartment window on the eastern edge of the city. I wouldn't be needing a career in real estate, after all. My dear aunt had bequeathed me her modest, mortgage-free bungalow in Scarborough, along with a generous investment bond. I owed it to myself to use this gift as a springboard and write my novel; Gustav had done it on less. I looked forward to more conversations with him over the next few months, for as long as his lungs held out.

I couldn't resist looking up my social media accounts to bask in my revenge on Bob. Twitter wouldn't download—a clogged feed, I was sure. I tried Facebook. Yes, my article was doing fine: over a thousand "likes," five hundred and fifty-three "shares", and tons of comments that I dared not open and get lost in at this moment—perhaps, I'd save them for review tonight, over a tall beer. There was also one friend request.

I opened the friend request: Maureen Fisher.

As I hit "accept," something told me that my world was about to change again.

LONG ROAD BACK

"Goodbye, Justine," Bob says. "I'll be in touch."

She hugs him one last time—it will be a while before she feels the nearness of a man again, the mingled smell of aftershave and sweat. She hopes that this time the lean period will be shorter.

"Go now, before I get all bleary eyed," she replies.

He leaves her at the door and hurries to his car, anxious to exit before the doubts appear. His posture is upright and his clothes well-laundered. He has a purpose now: Sue would insist on good grooming—younger women usually do. And all the other things, too, like paying attention, cooking dinner, being romantic, and being on call whenever the sexual urge beckoned. Justine sighs— it had been so different between them. They had spent time talking, drinking wine by the fireplace, and he had cried in her arms when he recalled his failed marriage, the lost children, and the drop in social standing due to the economic toll of a divorce. And when they made love, it had been long and lingering—she'd taught him that. Wham, bang, thank you, and let's do it all over again in half an hour—did not work for her. Foreplay for at least an hour, gentle stroking, and a climax that was withheld for hours only to be plunged into with a force that moved heaven and earth was something he had learned from her and could now gift to any woman who desired Tantric sex.

Yet when he had first come to her place—a discreet invitation from her at the art society meeting—he had been dishevelled, his hair grown over the shoulder, and he hadn't shaved in a week. Unkempt, was more the word. He'd drunk a lot, too—some men did in the early stages, and she ensured there was always a bottle or two of wine around the house. It was good in the beginning to get a man to talk, get it all off his chest.

They did not sleep together until their third meeting; he was willing to jump into the sack sooner, to get lost in her and blot out his problems, but she knew he needed time to unburden. He climaxed too soon that first time, just slumped into limpidness after a hurried rush of thrusting, more in wanting to transfer his pain than in giving her pleasure. She let him wear himself out before introducing him to Tantric for Beginners, something she had mastered over the last fifteen years. It was her life mission.

She shuts the front door and goes into the living room. She tries the lock several times to ensure the door *is* locked—an old habit from many years ago. The fireplace is empty; soon it will be summer. She draws the blinds—it's a grey day outside. Bob had come to her in the late fall; his cure had taken five months.

Eva jumps off the staircase leading to the bedroom and slides onto her lap, and Justine strokes the cat's mane. Eva, once a feral cat, stuck in the fence when Justine found her and took her in. Eva now eight years old and a darling, almost human, who sleeps in the main bedroom, even if there are men in her mistress' bed. Eva always sleeps in the bedroom—a pre-condition for all men sleeping with Justine Mahoney. She laughs as she recalls Jim, one of her lovers, who had an allergy to cat fur and got so stuffed up he had to take antihistamines before entering her bedroom.

She picks up the photographs of the recent trip Bob and she had made to Florence—it was time to put him in the archives. She pauses opposite the old writing desk in her study, an inheritance from her deceased parents. This is the hardest part, going through the history. Yet she knows she has to do it. This is the only way *she* will heal.

The album is in many parts. In fact, there are about six books strung together with a thick cord running through them. It is so heavy with photographs, letters, and other memorabilia that she staggers while walking into the living room to place it on the coffee table. She sits on the pine floor and turns the worn pages.

Bob will go in front, as he is the most recent. She removes the picture taken on the first day he arrived at her doorstep—yes, he was badly in need of repair then. The picture taken on the morning after their first night in bed looks better; he is relaxed, though introspective. Two months later and he is getting the hang of giving and prolonging—look at that smile of confidence on his face! He looks anticipatory in the picture taken on the way to the airport when they were bound for Italy—it was important to get him out of his environment and let him see there was another world out there from the one that shouted "DIVORCE" in big letters. And boy, isn't he smug in this one taken at the Piazzalle Michaelangelo the day before they left Florence, overlooking the red city after a couple of glasses of wine and a heavy meal of pasta and gelato?

She sighs as she remembers him telling her three weeks ago, soon after their return, that he had gone to Sue's birthday party. Sue, whom he had always had a crush on at work, but whom he had stayed clear of as he was married at the time. Sue, who after the party, had invited him to her parents' cottage. Today, when he had come over, Justine sensed it was over between them. She shakes her head and looks at the picture of them on the Ponte Vecchio the day they arrived in Florence. He had been shy and awkward when she had kissed him in public in the middle of that famed bridge—a thing all lovers did. On the way back from the Piazzale Michaelangelo, two weeks later, heady with Chianti, he had returned the honour by grabbing her at the same spot on the old bridge and forcing his lips down on hers. She had felt the effort and concentration he put into the kiss, not the giving and abandonment she had offered him the first time—but at least he had tried. Perhaps, he had been practicing for Sue.

The phone rings.

"Hello, Justine?" It was Iris from the horticultural society. "Are you coming to the show?"

"Yes, I was planning to. I said so at the last meeting."

"Thank God! Marge is in crisis."

"What's happened?" Justine hated Marge, the president, with her bossy ways.

"Well, her husband finally gave her the heave ho!"

"About time." She got goose bumps around Gregory Townsend, with his tall figure and flowing grey hair. Greg, a retired college dean, was courteous and a gentleman, even when Marge was short and snappy with him.

"Marge is in counseling and on the verge of a breakdown. We've told her to leave the show to us. Can you help with the judging?"

"Of course." As Iris chatters on with the details, Justine's mind is only half alert. She pictures Greg free at last. The poor man must be lost, after nearly thirty years of marriage to that horrible woman. Her mind drifts to the day she saw him trailing the group of women in the greenhouse. He picked up a rose that had fallen on the floor. He gently brushed the dirt-streaked petals, without dislodging any, then he held it against the light. Finally seeing her, he extended the rose. "It becomes you— beauty is so fragile, isn't it? We have to preserve every bit of it while we can." Then he blushed, bowed, and hurried after the women where Marge, in the lead, was holding forth on the finer points of growing orchids in northern climes. Justine realized that day that Gregory was special, unlike the other men she had known.

When Iris finally signs off after exacting a promise from her to attend the following day's emergency meeting to "tie up loose ends", Justine goes into her kitchen and pours a cup of tea. She looks out of the window dreamily. The garden is just spouting Scylla and Daffodils; the perennials will be out next month. She times her garden, in which she now spends so many hours in the day, to have flowers in bloom continuously between April and October—a dormant hobby re-ignited after taking early retirement from a college professor's career that had spanned twenty-five years.

She walks through the house and looks at the upgrades she has made over the years: the front doors, the new flooring, and the remodeled guest washroom. Also, the new roof and the re-paved driveway. Improvements she budgets for frugally, now that she is down to a pension. The car, her last large purchase before retirement, sits in the driveway, and she hopes it will last her a good fifteen years with careful maintenance. She pauses in front of the wall-to-ceiling mirror in the alcove by the front door, added five years ago, and appraises herself. The hair is still dark brown; the grey flecks are kept at bay with regular dyeing. Angular cheeks, eyes still vivacious but dulling into matronly kindness, a firm bust line kept from sagging with a push-up bra, and long legs, still firm. Exercising at least five times a week at the gym with a swim to round things off would account for her physical well-being at the age of fifty. That and good sex with younger men. She sighs as the thought crosses her mind. Yes, they had all been younger men ever since her one and only marriage. Bob had been ten years younger than her—one couldn't blame him if Sue, five years younger than him, had finally turned his head.

The album beckons and she places her teacup beside it and turns the pages, going back in time.

Back through the pages to Paul, whom she had met at the amateur theatre club three years ago. He had been the lead actor and extremely handsome. He was also charming and a poseur. Always ready with a great comeback line, always upbeat. When they found him, drunk and passed out in the alleyway behind the theatre on opening night, she knew he had a problem he was concealing from the world. He came under her wing soon after that. When they broke up a year later, he was drinking less, delivering his lines flawlessly, and not going into those dreadful sulks that alternated with his elevated moods. He still phones, just before a show, when he is full of the jitters and contemplating the bottle. Talking to her prevents him succumbing, he says.

As she delves deeper into the album, the pictures of her with men show a younger, more aggressive Justine. More daring outfits, shorter hair, heavier make-up. "I was good then," she mutters to herself, draining her teacup.

Lawrence came along in the early nineties. A businessman, her first from the rational world, and a challenge she wanted to take on. He had impeccable table manners, thanks to the many client dinners he'd had practice with. He ran through money, his, hers, and others', as if there were no tomorrow. They had been going steady for six months when he called her one night saying he was going to be lying low for awhile in a foreign country. The next day, the newspapers broke the infamous securities scandal where Lawrence's firm was accused of defrauding investors to the tune of millions of dollars as the recession had deepened. She never heard from him after that. Well, she couldn't save them all!

She rises and goes into the kitchen once more. There is something she needs to do. She takes a deep breath and picks up the phone. Her palms are clammy—this has never happened in a long time with her men. She dials Gregory Townsend's cell phone number which Marge doesn't know she has. She is relieved when his voicemail greeting comes on. She leaves a message.

"Hello Greg, I heard the news. I'm very proud of you. This is the first step in your long journey back. Call me if you need to talk." She replaces the receiver and recalls the unexpected call he gave her a few weeks ago.

"Hi Justine? Oh, hi! This is Gregory Townsend—you know, Marge's husband—from the horticultural society?"

"Oh, yes, Gregory, what a surprise! Thank you for the rose the other day."

"Er, yes, my pleasure. Justine… I know we've only met a few times before, but I wanted to discuss a delicate matter with someone impartial. Do you have a few minutes?"

"Of course!" For Gregory Townsend? She'd give him a few hours! He'd never called her before.

"It's about Marge and me. You see, it's complicated…"

"You can talk to me, Greg." It must have been the gentleness in her voice. He started unburdening himself. Thirty years of living with a bitch of a wife came out in waves of principled and controlled speech. She admired his reserve and poise as he recounted the aggressive public put-downs, the nagging, the demands for money, the denial of sex for non-performance in other areas.

"…And so, you see, I am in an untenable situation. My sanity is at stake here," Gregory Townsend concluded.

"*Leave her*, Greg." That was all she offered, with finality.

"Do you think that is a justifiable action?"

"Based on what you've told me I think it is. You've put up with too much."

"Are you sure?"

"Absolutely."

He thanked her and rang off. She had quickly saved his cell phone number which had shown up on her call display.

Now, he is acting on her advice, and she feels good.

She returns to the album on the coffee table, spins a few lovers back, and lands up in the year 1985. A pivotal year. The year she met Mohandas.

Her life had been a blank in the intervening years since her marriage ended—no relationships, fear of relationships, a couple of desperate, sweat-soaked one-night stands that had gone nowhere. When the AIDS crisis broke, she decided to give up on blind dates too. She was well and truly stuck. Then Doris, her colleague at the community college, had invited her to an evening of meditation and eastern cooking. Doris was famous for her theme parties. A special guest had been invited: Dr. Mohandas Ramakrishna, recently arrived from India and in charge of a school for eastern arts down in the west end of the city.

When they settled in a circle on the floor in Doris's large living room, Justine had trouble keeping her eyes off Mohandas. Fortyish, thin as a reed, yet supple, with an aquiline nose and a tanned body, Mohandas was dressed in a flowing white shirt, open at the chest that spouted a luxurious growth of hair. He was mesmerizing as he led them through a guided meditation, his voice deep and commanding, shepherding them through the labyrinthine world of the semi-conscious. Later, he got onto his guest talk which was on Tantra, and, by extension, sex. The women in the group giggled as he spoke about withholding ejaculation for hours and having no other objective in sight to lovemaking than pure pleasure. For the first time in a long time she was wet between her legs by the time they adjourned to a sumptuous feast of samosas, pakoras, idlis, matter paneer, aloo gobi and... and... Justine lost track of the other delicacies that Doris had ordered from the neighbourhood Indian restaurant.

During the break, Justine decided to be bold. "Teach me Tantra," she said, sidling up to Mohandas and looking him in the eye. It had felt good, plucking the courage after all these barren years, but she felt compelled and propelled towards him. He looked at her with his dark features inscrutable. "You could be a teacher yourself," he said. "But first you must learn. It is not easy, it requires opening yourself and taking responsibility for your own pleasure."

"I'll learn. Show me."

"All right then. Let's meet after classes at the center Thursdays at eight p.m. Here is my card." Then he walked away casually to make conversation with the rest of the group.

And teach her he did. After the first three classes that had focused on meditation and deep breathing to connect with one's pleasure bases, he took her through foreplay that had her rolling in abandon. The part about prolonging ejaculation was true, she discovered; they made love for hours and hours. "Where have I been all these years?" was a question she often asked when she lay satiated and sweaty in his arms.

When her new fall teaching schedule came out, she had to lecture on Thursday evenings, so she tried to change their date but found out Mohandas was booked on other days. She soon discovered that he had a woman for every night of the week. She was hurt and angry, yet realized this was going to be an eventuality. When she called Doris and vented on the phone, her friend listened at first, but concluded firmly that Mohandas was too delicious to give up.

"What do you mean?" Justine shouted, angry at Doris's lack of empathy.

"Well, honey, I wouldn't give you my weekly slot with him for the world! Barry and I have finally got it together, thanks to my Monday's with the Master."

On the last Thursday she spent with Mohandas, she took him by surprise by mounting him earlier than usual and riding him like he was a disposable toy. Sucking his seed into her before he could go through his suppression routine, she rode him till he shriveled and fell out of her.

Exhausted, he rolled over and said, "By Jove! You have become the master—you can teach others now. Just don't do this in anger."

She realized then that her recovery would be a longer road back.

She flips Mohandas' picture over and pauses. Mohandas was a turning point, when she came into her own and decided to save other men—men who had screwed up their marriages and relationships by being traditional and self-absorbed. Tantra became her mission in life at that point and gave her a focus in the area of love and relationships. Tantra served to deflect her emptiness and sublimate her anger into service.

That's why she had been able to restore Bob and Paul and all the others who had come after Mohandas. But they were all lesser mortals than Gregory Townsend. Gregory was becoming a new turning point. She remembers last weekend when she was needled into addressing the guests at Doris' pre-March Break soirée.

"All you sex lovers! A little speech before dessert, from a devout adherent to Tantra and the arts of eastern sex— our very own—Justine!" Doris was waving a champagne glass and everyone was a bit drunk.

The women gathered eagerly while their husbands hung in the background, somewhat embarrassed. Gregory was standing by the fireplace, unsure whether to leave or stay. Justine, a couple of glasses of wine warming her belly, launched into the art of breathing, of aligning energy centers. She looked at Gregory as she got deeper into her description. He held her gaze right through her explanation of how to delay ejaculation by avoiding stimulating a man's Frenulum, or by applying the Perineum Press.

"Poppycock!" Marge burst out, downing her glass. "Men can't hold it that long no matter what we do. Christ, they can't even hold it until we climax!" A man guffawed then stopped as others hissed.

"Speak for yourself" Doris said laughing and squeezing her husband Barry's hand.

"Women, too, are responsible for male climaxes," Iris said, trying to add brevity to the discussion. There were muffled male growls of approval around the room. The men began escaping into the dining room where, much to their relief, dessert was being served.

Gregory was still standing by the fireplace as Justine passed by him into the dining room. He must have been too embarrassed to follow the men after Marge's revelation.

"You are a bold woman," he said. "I'm proud of you."

Her face flushed, and she tried to hide it by being flippant. "Sorry, a hot flash, I think."

"You don't have to apologize," he said, following her to the dessert table." You should be happy for the life you have."

Would she dare go after Gregory, now that he was available? He was classy. Well, she'd had classy men in her life—once upon a time, long ago—long before Mohandas. That is the part of the album she has not opened in over twenty years. That part of her life still makes her anxious in shopping malls and in other public places, and has her trying the front door several times after locking it.

She rises, goes into the kitchen, and gets food for Eva. She places it in a bowl by her feet and takes the animal in her lap. She needs another living soul to draw from for what she has to do next. Taking a breath, she opens the last of the bound books in the album.

Staring at her are two photographs. In one is a man, handsome, thirtyish, and dressed in a well-tailored suit. His eyes are luminous, and to this day she feels his tug. He is leaning against a two-door BMW sports car. Carl Preminger was dashing, no doubt about it. From the night he'd picked her up at the university graduation ball, to their whirlwind romance, he'd been nothing but a dream. He was a great dancer, a long-distance runner, and had inherited his father's auto parts business. Still in a dream, she married him six months later.

Then the dream ended.

She slaved for him and tried to meet his every need as a good wife should. All she wanted from him was tenderness and for the romantic dream to continue. He reciprocated by rationing his lovemaking soon after the honeymoon. Then he started staying late at the office and going on golfing trips with his buddies on weekends.

The second photograph is of her evidence picture taken at the police station: an eye badly battered, clothes torn, lips swollen, dried blood drooling from her mouth. She trembles as she recalls the day, a year into her marriage.

"You are late again. Couldn't you call?" She was tired of keeping dinner warm and was angling for a fight. "Which chick is it this time?"

He was hanging up his coat, silent, not really caring anymore. He lit a cigarette, walked over to the liquor cabinet, and poured himself a scotch. He didn't offer her a glass of wine like he did in the old days, just over a year ago. He always drank hard liquor, not a lot, but regularly. She'd never seen him drunk, but he'd always hovered at the edges of a smoldering rage.

He eyed her, toying with his drink, watching the ice swish back and forth. "If you want to know, it's Brittany."

His new secretary. She was shocked that he was so brazen about it.

"She's a hot pursuit. Unlike you." He continued to play with his glass, taking occasional sips.

"Is that why you married me?" she said.

"Women should know how to drive their men crazy with desire."

"You tricked me into marrying you. I never saw this misogyny when we were dating."

"Why show the dark side, eh?" He laughed quietly to himself. "You've changed yourself. Got all housewifely."

"What have I done wrong, Carl?"

"Nothing, that's what—nothing. You do nothing for me now, either. I can't get it off with you anymore."

"You bastard!"

"Now, when you get angry, you somehow look more interesting. Go on, hit me—that might be more fun than sitting in a corner in that frumpy dress."

She ran at him and pounced. He moved quick, putting the glass down and sidestepping so that she slipped and crashed into the stereo. Then his hand was on her hair, and he was dragging her across the floor. He started beating her, slaps to the face, on her legs. He was tearing her clothes, her panties, and spreading her legs. She fought him but could only see his seething angry face creasing into a slight smile. He hit her really hard, and she felt her jaw break. The next thing he was inside her, hard—he'd not been like that in a long time. "This is how I want you," was all she heard before blacking out.

When she came to, he had tied her to their bed, and he forced himself into her repeatedly as she struggled and squirmed. "There is no pleasure without the hunt and the struggle. I shouldn't have got married," he told her by way of explanation as he penetrated her dry insides for the fourth time that evening.

She left later that night as he snored on the sofa, by biting off the thongs that had fastened her to the bed. She reported the incident to the police, a restraining order was issued, and divorce proceedings got underway. The trauma has lived with her ever since. After the divorce, he stalked her. He'd call her up at night and say that he was enjoying the chase now more than before they got married. She lived in terror, triple-locking her doors, not going out unless accompanied by a friend.

She turns the album to the picture of the car crash, ten years ago. Carl went off the road one Christmas eve. He, and the woman he was with, died on the spot.

But Justine still checks and double-checks her doors at night.

Somehow, the images are not frightening anymore. That is a relief. Re-visiting the album has helped. Perhaps the men who had come and gone since Carl have taken some of the edge out of that traumatic experience. Perhaps she is ready for a *real* man again, not the hapless ones she has been practicing with. Carl hadn't been a real man, either—just the illusion of one. She wonders how he would have behaved towards her if she had practiced the art of Tantra on him—but Carl had been and gone before Mohandas came into her life and put it on its current path.

She closes the album. A dried flower falls out from among the pages. The rose that Gregory had given her that day in the greenhouse. She gently places it back in the album, but its petals crumble into a fine dust. She picks up the scraps, puts them back within the pages, and presses the album shut; that's all she's got of Gregory, for now, no photographs, not yet. She puts the album away, ensuring nothing falls out this time.

She cradles Eva in her arms. "It looks like we are destined for a lonely life, my love," she whispers. Eva purrs in response and snuggles closer to her mistress. For once it would be nice to be vulnerable again, to put it all on the line like she had done for Carl, even if it meant another disappointment and a tsunami of hurt. She is getting tired of being the clinical saviour of men, emotionally buttoned up, yet sexually un-zipped.

The phone rings.

Oh, leave me alone—I just want to be alone. But she has been alone for too long, and she instinctively reaches for the receiver.

"Hello, Justine? It's Greg… Gregory. I got your message."

Her pulse quickens, she squeezes Eva who looks up knowingly and purrs aloud. This was no longer a clinical discussion with a wounded man in need of relief. A force is propelling her to an inevitable rendezvous with destiny after what had been a long detour. She has crossed her limbo.

"Why hello, Gregory. It's nice of you to call…"

ABOUT THE AUTHOR

Shane Joseph began writing as a teenager living in Sri Lanka and has never stopped. From an early surge of short stories and radio play scripts, to humorous corporate skits, travelogues, case studies and technical papers, then novels, more short stories, and essays, he continues to pursue the three pages-a-day maxim and keeps writer's block at bay.

His career stints include: stage and radio actor, pop musician, encyclopaedia salesman, lathe machine operator, airline executive, travel agency manager, vice president of a global financial services company, software services salesperson, project manager, editor, business owner, and management consultant.

Self-taught, with four degrees under his belt obtained through distance education, Shane is an avid traveller and has visited one country for every year of his life. He fondly recalls incidents during his travels as real lessons he could never have learned in school: husky driving in Finland with no training, trekking the Inca Trail in Peru through an unending rainstorm, hitch-hiking in Australia without a map, escaping a wild elephant in Zambia, and being stranded without money in Denmark are some of his memories.

Shane is a graduate of the Humber School for Writers in Toronto and studied under the mentorship of Giller Prize and Canadian Governor General's Award winning author David Adams Richards. His published works include the novels *Redemption in Paradise* (2004), *After the Flood* (2009), *The Ulysses Man* (2011) and *In the Shadow of the Conquistador* (2015). His previously published short story collections are *Fringe Dwellers* (2008) and *Paradise Revisited* (2013). His short fiction has appeared in literary journals and anthologies internationally. His blog is widely syndicated.

After immigrating twice, raising a family, building a career, and experiencing life's many highs and lows, Shane has carved out a niche in Cobourg, Ontario with his wife, Sarah, where he continues to work, write stories, and strum his guitar.

More details on Shane's work and blog can be found on his website at www.shanejoseph.com.